THE INCREDIBLE
TIGER-MAN

ADAM PFEFFER

iUniverse LLC
Bloomington

THE INCREDIBLE TIGER-MAN

iUniverse books may be ordered through booksellers or by contacting:

iUniverse
1663 Liberty Drive
Bloomington, IN 47403
www.iuniverse.com
1-800-Authors (1-800-288-4677)

Because of the dynamic nature of the Internet, any web addresses or links contained in this book may have changed since publication and may no longer be valid. The views expressed in this work are solely those of the author and do not necessarily reflect the views of the publisher, and the publisher hereby disclaims any responsibility for them.

Any people depicted in stock imagery provided by Thinkstock are models, and such images are being used for illustrative purposes only.

Certain stock imagery © Thinkstock.

ISBN: 978-1-4917-0519-3 (sc)
ISBN: 978-1-4917-0520-9 (e)

Printed in the United States of America.

iUniverse rev. date: 8/23/2013

For Leonard and Anita

We have made a covenant with death,
and with hell are we at agreement.

ISAIAH 28:15

INTRODUCTION

HOWEVER BIZARRE IT MAY SEEM, there are documented cases around the world of people believing they have transformed into an animal or display both human and animal characteristics. The following story deals with those beliefs, which extend back to the earliest days of man, and remain with us in modern-day society.

Today, however, we consider these ancient beliefs to be rare psychiatric conditions associated with serial killers and psychosis. The following story also deals with shamanism and totem animals, which have played a part in primitive and nature-based cultures.

There are many terms associated with these beliefs, both ancient and modern, and it seems particularly useful to go through them before beginning the story.

First of all, in modern society, there's clinical lycanthropy. This is the psychiatric disorder that involves the delusional belief that a person has transformed into an animal. It is named after the mythical condition of lycanthropy, which dealt with people turning into werewolves. *Zoanthropy* is also used for a person who has turned into an animal in general and not specifically a wolf.

Therianthropy is the term used for any transformation of a human into another animal form. It's also used for any person who displays both human and animal characteristics, either as part of mythology or as a part of spirituality.

The common form is lycanthropy, which is the technical term for the transformation of a person into an animal. Some people frown upon using this term for anything other than a wolf transformation, since the word comes from the Greek for *lycos* or "wolf" and *anthropos* or "man." Though the word specifically refers to a change into wolf form, it can be used to refer to a human changing to any non-human animal form.

In medical terms, lycanthropy is not used only for the human-to-wolf transformation, but for the shape-shifting experience in general. Medical literature from 2004 lists over thirty published cases of lycanthropy, only a few having to do with wolf or dog themes. The lists include humans being transformed into cats, horses, birds and tigers, with even frogs and bees included. A 1989 case study involved one person who supposedly experienced a serial transformation, changing from human to dog to horse, and then to cat, before returning to human form after treatment.

The origin of the term, lycanthropy, comes from Greek mythology and the story of Lycaon, who transformed into a wolf as result of eating human flesh. There is another story from Pliny the Elder in Roman times, who quoting Euanthes, says a man of the Anthus family, having been brought to a lake in Arcadia, swam across and was transformed into a wolf for nine years. If he had attacked no human being in that time, he was free to swim back and resume his former shape.

In later years, it was believed malignant sorcerers and even Christian saints, such as St. Patrick and St. Natalis, had the power to transform humans into wild beasts. According to St. Thomas Aquinas, "all angels, good and bad have the power of transmutating our bodies."

But it was shamans who used potions and ritual to contact and become animals themselves, something modern psychiatry would frown upon as a form of mental illness.

When people believe they change into a animal form through the process of theriomorphosis, the term clinical lycanthropy is usually used. These therians or therianthropes, which means *beast-man*, believe they have the power of shape-shifting into some wild animal, and these beliefs have been a part of shamanism or totemism, as well as the myths in Celtic, Norse and Native American cultures.

Some say a person identifying with an animal is somewhat similar to gender dysphoria and transsexuality, and is known as species dysphoria and transspeciesism. The species of non-human animal with which a therian identifies with is called that person's *theriotype* or *phenotype*.

Ethnologist Ivar Lissner theorized that identification with animals goes back to cave paintings, which he says were actually attempts by shamans to acquire the mental and spiritual aspects of various beasts.

Other authors say that stories of werewolves and vampires may have been used to explain serial killings in earlier days.

These beliefs and fears associated with werewolves and other animal transformations, however, survive in modern-day society. In the late 1990s, for example, man-eating wolf attacks in India caused frightened people to believe they were the work of werewolves. Such fears are the basis of the following story, a story based on legend and fact.

It is a story that lingers in the recesses of our brains and has endured through the past centuries of our existence. It may be a story well remembered as our dependence on Nature diminishes bringing about a detachment that could well transform the entire human race.

FLORIDA
August 2013

1

KOLAK

A PIERCING SCREAM ECHOED THROUGH the darkness, soared through the empty streets, and faded into the sullen, gray morning. Those who had heard the curdling cry shifted uneasily under their blankets, while others cuddled closer to their slumbering loved ones, while still others, nervously glanced at the time, and either decided to lie awake with their senses riveted to the drifting breeze or fumbled their way to the nearest light switch with the intention of beginning their day somewhat earlier than planned. A few rushed to the window, peering into the enveloping darkness, straining to see something, anything, that might allay their fears and assist them in rationally explaining the depraved undertakings of a city cloaked in shadow.

As the misty light of the grim morning settled in the air, the low moaning of sirens could be heard, soothing the terrified and stimulating the curious. The sirens were accompanied by the insistent barking of dogs resounding through the air, causing many to contemplate the terrible incident that had apparently taken place behind the veil of darkness.

Another shrill scream slashed through the pale light, and was quickly rejoined by the moaning police cars, which having found the source of the distress, screeched to a halt.

"Oh, my God!" wailed a woman staring at the body clinging to the blood-spattered sidewalk. "Dear God!"

The morning light, meanwhile, drifted through the air, resolutely driving the darkness further west, its actions seemingly aided by the urgent, flashing lights of the police cars. In the distance, a thin fog obscured the tops of the gigantic buildings that huddled together on this island that was a part of New York City. Down below, four police officers hurriedly emerged from their cars, one of them approaching the sobbing woman.

"Did you see anything?" the officer asked.

She looked at him as if his question was so horrifying it crossed the bounds of common decency. "God, no," she replied with a great sense of relief. "Dear God, thank God, nothing at all."

The officer nodded, inquired when she had first discovered the body, and then began writing down any relevant details. Meanwhile, the other officers stood over the body and gazed at the deep slashes, the severely torn skin, and the enormous amount of scarlet blood staining both the shredded clothing and the dirty sidewalk.

"Geez, he was goddamned ripped apart," murmured one of the officers.

"Must have been some sort of animal," said another. "We'd better find out if any of the zoos are reporting any escaped creatures."

As they stood there, more and more people began to venture from their secure abodes to the streets below, fearing the worst, and yet, hoping to confirm the actuality of their wildest nightmares. The crowd began to swell, and soon, the gawking mass of people beheld with their own eyes what their minds had presented as a realistic possibility of what had occurred in the midst of darkness.

"Oh my God, there's a wild animal on the loose," someone murmured. The crowd shifted, continuing to stare at the mangled corpse, and then the police officers became angry and attempted to force them back away from the crime scene.

"Maybe it was a dog," someone said, to which others began whispering their disdain. "No dog is capable of doing that much damage," answered one of them. "Whatever it was had claws, sharp as knives."

The remark caused another shudder of terror, and then the officers began shouting once again. "Don't you understand this is a crime scene?" one of them said. "And we can't have it compromised in any way."

As the people were once again pushed back, the officers began stretching plastic yellow tape around the area where the motionless body lay. Another siren now filled the air, a shrill, resonant groaning, and then a white van suddenly appeared and pulled up alongside the police cars.

Two men and a woman in uniforms emerged from the vehicle and hurried to the body. They studied the body for a moment, frowned, made a half-hearted attempt to examine him, and then rushed back to the van. They soon returned with a long, white sheet that they carefully draped over the mutilated remains.

"Can't do anything for this one," said one of the men to the officers. "The morgue will have to pick him up." He then walked back to the van, which, after several minutes, suddenly roared to life, and sped off into the distance.

It was a few seconds later that another car rushed up the street, a dark sedan, which also halted next to the police cars. A man in a dark suit, graying at the temples, with a gnarled look of one accustomed to great horrors, sauntered toward the yellow tape. Another man in a dark suit followed close behind.

They glanced at the body, bent down to examine the deep gashes, and then began seeking eyewitnesses. In the midst of this renewed activity, several other vehicles appeared, rushing down the street.

One of the men turned to look and then simply shook his head. "Well, here they come," he murmured. "The damned buzzards."

In a matter of seconds, the great throng was met by an onrush of microphones, cameras, and tape recorders. The crowd watched as the reporters, representing television, newspapers and radio, leaned against the yellow tape and began shouting their questions.

"Are there any suspects?" one of them asked. "Did anybody see anything?"

"At what time did the attack take place?"

The detective with the gray-flecked hair, who still wore a somber expression, frowned as he approached the glaring lights of the television cameras. "It seems as if he was attacked by some sort of animal," he grumbled. "We're checking to see if any animals from the zoos or nearby sanctuaries have been reported missing."

"What kind of animal are we talking about?" a female reporter with a microphone shouted.

"I can't answer that," the detective replied. "We'll let you know." He was about to turn back toward the corpse, when he heard a voice from behind the police cars.

"It was a tiger," the voice said.

The crowd turned, almost simultaneously, as a dark-haired man wearing tan clothing that he had seemingly slept in, moved slowly toward the yellow tape. "I've seen what damage they're capable of."

"Are you a zoologist?" asked one of the reporters, lunging toward him with a microphone.

"An anthropologist," he replied. "I study man, but I have seen what a tiger is capable of while in the jungles of Malaysia. It's not a very pretty sight, wouldn't you agree?"

"What's your name?"

He looked at the detective, calmly ran his fingers through his hair, and turned back toward the microphone. "Roger Kolak," he replied.

They studied his face, a rather haggard visage, with dark circles under his eyes, which looked weary from either stress or sleeplessness. He glanced at the reporter, and quickly looked down at the temporarily exposed corpse.

"*Panthera tigris*, I would say," he murmured into the nearby microphone. "They generally hunt at night."

"Did you see the creature?" asked the reporter.

Kolak slowly shook his head. "But I have seen the injuries they leave behind." He paused for a moment. "Many of them find human beings easy prey and become man-eaters."

The detective looked at him and motioned him past the reporters and inside the yellow-taped area. "Are you sure this is the work of a tiger, Mr. Kolak?" asked the detective, prompting him to take another look at the mangled body.

Kolak bent down and examined the wounds. "I would say definitely consistent with the wounds incurred in a tiger attack," he finally explained. "I have seen such victims many times before back in Malaysia."

"And you didn't actually see the creature?" the detective wanted to know.

"They know how to hide in the darkness and the shadows," Kolak replied. "He's probably quite a distance away from the site of the attack already."

The detective frowned. "If there's a tiger running around this city, I'm sure we'll hear about it soon enough. I wonder if you'd be able to stay here and help us with the creature when it's finally caught?"

"I'm sorry, but I must get going. I have a very important appointment with someone today, and I fear I'm late already."

"Do you have a number where I might contact you?"

"I'll get in touch with you, detective, as soon as I take care of that appointment. Is that sufficient?"

The detective nodded, and he watched as Kolak hunched beneath the yellow tape and disappeared into the dense crowd. He then turned back toward the bright lights of the television cameras and the shouting reporters, and grimaced.

"Roger, I'm so glad you're back."

The striking blonde female opened her arms and wrapped them around Kolak's torso. She had been waiting for him to return to her for months now, and as he embraced her, she felt a flare of tenderness rekindle within her heart, her soul, and radiate through her being. Theirs had been a relationship of passion, founded on mutual respect, causing an intense emotional upheaval in her life, in her system of beliefs and values, and had led to a pledge of eternal love and assurances of future matrimonial bliss. She stared into his eyes, touched his hands, and realized she was once again with the man she considered to be the one she would accompany through eternity.

"Gail, darling, how I love you so."

His reply drifted through her mind and awakened slumbering emotions she had hidden away for so long. Their lips met fervently, their bodies locked in passionate embrace, as the months of separation slowly melted away. She could feel the tears spilling from his eyes, the body trembling, and then, she, too, began to cry.

"Oh, look at us," she finally smiled. "We're a mess and people are beginning to stare."

"Let them," he replied. "Just holding you in my arms again is all that matters to me."

"But Roger, you haven't told me about your trip. I must know what kept you away from me for so long."

Her words produced a pained expression across his face, and then, suddenly, he began to cry once again. She watched in horror as he stood before her and bitterly wept.

"What is it, Roger?" she gasped. "What happened to you?"

After a few moments, he stopped crying, and looked at her with sorrow filling his eyes. "I really can't tell you right now, Gail," he said mysteriously. "But, just know, the thought of you filled my mind, my dreams, wherever I went. The glimmer of your eyes, the gentleness of your voice, kept me going when I feared all was lost. Some day, maybe, I'll be able to tell you all that occurred, but now is not that time. You see, even I have a hard time understanding it right now."

"But what about all we had promised each other? There were to be no secrets between us, nothing to disturb our undying love for each other. Roger, you promised to tell me everything, no matter the circumstances. After all, if we are to be married you must confide in me, whether or not it is bad or good. That is the foundation of a true partnership, one built on respect and trust."

He turned away, and frowned. "I doubt you would want to marry me after I tell you everything that has happened," he whispered. "It is a terrifying story, one that haunts me to this very day."

"You're not in any trouble, are you, my darling? I mean, there's nobody looking for you, is there, Roger?"

She could see him pausing for a moment, his head bowed in silence.

"They don't know it's me they are hunting for," he finally replied. "But they will soon enough, and that's why I must not see you again."

She frowned at the words, the tears emerging from her eyes. "But Roger, if you're in trouble, let me be the one to help you. I'll hide you, lie for you, and make sure no harm comes to you. Only you must tell me what you've done, what has happened. Only then can I really help you and advise you what to do."

He stammered for a moment, trying to decide what to say. "It was in Malaysia—"

"Oh, Roger, did you kill someone? But you're home now, in America, why should you still fear anyone looking for you here?"

"Because it's not over yet, Gail. Don't you understand? What happened there is not over yet—"

He looked at her and began to sob once again. She wrapped her arms around him, let him bury his head in her breasts, and then led him back to her apartment.

"We will be safe there," she said, "no matter who is looking for you. Then, maybe, you will tell me the entire story, and allow me to judge what to do next. But, please, Roger, you must trust me if I am to help you."

Gail. If she had only known he had always trusted her, from the very first time he had heard her speak, entranced by the gracefully nimble words that seemed to dance from her soft, warm lips.

"According to Darwin, man still bears the indelible stamp of his lowly origin," she was saying all those months ago, the glow of the dimmed lights reflected on her glass of wine. "But he says a far more perfect creature will emerge in the distant future."

"That's only because Darwin had never made your acquaintance," he had replied.

She laughed at the remark, took another sip of wine, and stared into his eyes. The glimmer of beauty glistened in her dazzling sapphire orbs.

"But don't you agree that the human creature is constantly developing?" she asked.

"We can do no worse than where we came from," he had said. "You see, our origins are founded upon violence and the fierce struggle to survive. From the primal apes, came a savage who delighted in torture, practiced bloody sacrifices, killed without remorse, exhibited periods of rage and hate, treated his women like slaves, coveted possessions both animate and inanimate, and was continually guided and haunted by the most arbitrary and puzzling superstitions that placed him above Nature and a slave to the heavens."

When he had finished, he was once again staring into those beautiful, gleaming eyes.

"Then can we ever rise above our origin?" she asked. "I mean, is there still hope for the human race?"

"That is what I hope to find out, my dear," he had replied. "Just what is the potential of the human soul? Is it doomed to damnation or capable of spiritual redemption?"

"I am hopeful it's the latter," she had said, sipping her wine. "You see, I remain optimistic about the human potential."

"Yes, but first we must fully understand from where we have come. That's why I chose to study cultural anthropology in the first place. You see, if humans passed from savagery to civilized beings, we must find out why and how and what parts of that primitive being survived."

Kolak looked up from his cup of coffee, and sighed, thinking about those distant times before he left for Malaysia. "Oh, Gail, don't you think I want to tell you everything that has occurred? But what is the point of scaring you when there is nothing that can be done to correct the situation. I am resigned to my fate, though it be the sentence of damnation handed down by an indifferent Being capricious in his abusive judgments."

"But I must know, Roger, what is it that tears at your soul? What is it that has been done to you?"

He sipped at his coffee, and leaned back in the chair he was sitting in, a sudden gloom overtaking his face. "Oh, it's too horrible, too incredible, to even begin to tell," he groaned. "If I thought that there was any way I could be helped, any way tragedy could be averted, I wouldn't hesitate to explain. But you must trust me, Gail, now is not the right time. You must have faith, enough for both of us that somehow everything will turn out for the best. That, somehow, there is a master plan guiding us in our chaotic wanderings."

She stared at him, a tear running down her cheek. "And what about us, Roger?" she finally asked. "Is there no longer any love, any bond, between us?"

"If only you knew how much I love you," he said. "But I can't pretend that everything is the way it was before. Oh, how I wish that I could! But you must know by now that I still love you as much, maybe even more, than I did before. Yet, I still must take into consideration the future of our lives. Yours as well as mine."

"Do you ever think you'll find what you're searching for?" she had asked him long before he had headed off to Malaysia.

"I found you, didn't I?" he had joked in reply. This was on the verge of the third millennium, the end of the twentieth century, and they were prepared to welcome the new age in each other's arms, hoping it would bring an end to human suffering and violence just as the Bible had promised. There were concerns about the new millennium, Y2K as it was called, but they disregarded the dire warnings and decided the world was about to experience the promises of harmony and earthly perfection. At least, that was what they had tried to convince themselves.

"Maybe our evolution will reach a new stage," she laughed, as they sat together discussing the momentous event. "Maybe Satan will finally be defeated once and for all."

"He will be if he ever tries to interfere with our love," he replied.

"But, seriously, Roger, things must improve in the new century, don't you think?"

"How could they not, my darling? The twentieth century was one of the most violent centuries known to the history of mankind, including two world wars, the indiscriminate slaughter of people based upon their religious beliefs, racial inequality and prejudice, and the beginning of the nuclear age with the bloody destruction of two Japanese cities. But through all this, we have survived and will continue to do so, just as our love for each other will continue to survive and to grow."

He remembered the way she looked at him, as if a world asunder could not disrupt their love, their passion, and then she took his hand and gently kissed it. "No matter what happens," she had said, "I will always be there for you, my darling."

Kolak thought about those words as he stared into the shadows of the room. She had pledged her love, her devotion, as the world hurtled onward into a new epoch, forever promising to stand beside him even in the worst of times. The worst of times had arrived, had engulfed him, and she was still there, standing beside him, encouraging him to struggle on . . .

He paused for a moment, and standing up, began walking toward the door. "I must leave now," he said as gently as possible. "The night is coming, and I must make sure it is a peaceful one."

She stood up, the tears flowing from her eyes, and ran toward him. "Oh, Roger, tell me what it all means? I must know."

"You will in time," he grimly replied. "And when you do, please have pity, my darling." He then opened the door, stepped outside, and hurried away into the shadows of the dim corridor.

2

ANOTHER VICTIM

HE WAS STARING INTO THE scorched pot and watching as the Malays deposited the items into the boiling water. Cowbane, hemlock, opium, aconite, poplar leaves, foxglove, nightshade, cinquefoil . . .

They were holding a dead bat and letting the blood trickle down into the deadly mixture. Then one of the murdered children from a nearby village was carried over. They carefully peeled the fat from its lifeless body and threw the ragged-edged chunks in . . .

There was a full moon overhead and he felt his limbs go numb and his body twisting and stretching until his eyes were tinged with a glowing yellow . . .

His mind wandered until he felt himself clawing and scratching, his nails digging deep into the skin of another human being. He couldn't control his actions, felt the voice inside him buried deep down the shaft of his throat, unable to cry out in fear, or in pain, or in remorse . . .

He could feel the other person's heart hammering inside his body, could feel the flecks of skin curling under his fingernails. And then a shot rang out. There was a burning sensation, a twinge of pain, and he turned and darted into a nearby alleyway . . .

"I think I got him. Damn, I got him."

On the Upper East Side of Manhattan, a man in his thirties stood near a motionless body, a gun in his hand, gazing at the opening of an alleyway that plunged into the shadows.

Those few people nearby, not sufficiently reassured, stared at the mutilated body lying in the glistening puddle of blood, the scene grimly lit by the glow of the streetlight. The sound of the sirens steadily grew louder, and soon, they could see the flashing lights of the police cars glaring in the darkness. When the police officers finally emerged, they were directed toward the blood-soaked body.

"It was an animal of some kind," the man holding the gun attempted to explain. "I fired a few shots and he ran into that alleyway. It looked like a damned tiger, for god's sake."

The officers listened to the man and then hurried into the darkened opening, slowly disappearing into the narrow alleyway. They shambled down the dim corridor, their guns ready to fire, carefully peering into the darkness.

When they reached an intersecting passage, they halted for a moment, glanced around the corner, and spotted another body lying amidst the shadows. One of the officers withdrew a flashlight, and directed the beam of light toward the silent form. A naked male body, covered in blood, lay motionless upon the dirty cement.

"Geez," said one of the officers, "looks like he was taken right out of bed."

Kolak groaned, his hand held firmly against his forehead. He opened his eyes, saw that he was completely naked, and realized he had not been dreaming. But how could it not have been a nightmare?

A nightmare, damn it, nothing more than a nightmare. He blinked his eyes and slid one of his hands across the layer of blood enveloping his arm. He still couldn't believe it. The worst nightmares are the ones that actually come true, he muttered to himself. He looked down at his fingernails, and saw that they were caked with blood and skin. The only thing he could do was to try to get back to his apartment.

He would stand up, stagger down the street, and proceed to erase any memories of what had occurred. Then he could think, think hard, and decide what to do next. He would find out how to prevent his nightmares from becoming full-blown reality. There had to be a way to prevent it.

Sitting up, he rested his head in his blood-soaked hands, trying to gather the strength to rise to his feet. He tightened his muscles, balancing on the balls of his feet, and then rolled backwards onto the pavement.

"Hey, mister, don't try to move," said a voice to his right. "We'll take care of everything, don't you worry. The ambulance will be here before you know it and they'll fix you up as good as new, don't you worry about a thing. Just don't move too much until we find out what's wrong with you."

Kolak looked up, noticed it was a police officer, and attempted to sit up once again. "There's nothing wrong with me, officer," he groaned, trying to remain as calm as possible. "I'll be all right."

The officer stared down at Kolak's blood-spattered body and frowned. "You just stay there and wait for the ambulance to come and then we'll see how well you are," he said. "Anyway, it looks like you caught a bullet in your shoulder."

Kolak glanced at his right shoulder, and could see the lips of the wound protruding from the skin. Blood oozed from the wound, and trickled down his right arm.

"Funny, I didn't realize I've been shot," he muttered.

"Must have been near that animal when that guy was firing his gun," replied the officer. "But I wouldn't worry, it doesn't look too bad. Now you just rest until the ambulance gets here."

The officer then nodded to his partner, who hurried back down the alleyway.

The officer had his back turned now, wasn't watching, when Kolak tried again to struggle to his feet . . .

He felt his heart pounding, his mind racing, as he slowly stood up. He had to get back to his apartment. *Had to.* It was no good just sitting there and allowing them to capture him. He had to escape. He would think about what to do next once he was far away and they had given up looking for him. It was the only way . . .

"Hey, I told you not to move," said the officer. "Now you sit back down and wait for the ambulance."

"You don't understand, officer, I must get back to my apartment." He was so groggy and confused he didn't even realize he was telling the police officer his plan of escape.

"Apartment? You don't move, mister, until the ambulance comes and takes you to the hospital. You'll see, everything will work out just fine—"

Before the officer could finish, Kolak staggered forward, shoving the officer to the ground. *Now he had to escape.* He clattered down the alleyway, gasping for breath, and when he finally reached the opening, he lunged forward and fell to the sidewalk, landing only a few feet from the mangled body lying in the glare of the streetlight.

Must escape, he kept muttering to himself. *Must escape.* He could hear his labored breathing echoing in his ears, and then attempting to move his legs, his eyes closed and his movements eventually halted.

The man who had fired the shots at the animal watched as he fell to the pavement, stunned by his presence. "I didn't know he had grabbed someone else," he explained to an officer. "I only saw the snarling creature, I swear. I never would have fired my gun if I had seen him there."

"No one's blaming you," replied the officer. "We just want to know exactly what happened and get to the bottom of all this."

"Well . . . as I told you, it was an animal of some kind . . . a tiger or something like it," stammered the man.

In the distance, they could hear the sound of a siren whining in the night.

"You didn't notice this man at any time?" asked the officer.

The man looked down at the naked figure, and stammered once again. "I never saw him, I swear. All I saw was that animal, that tiger, or whatever the hell it was, snarling and growling as he ripped apart that body you see over there."

They looked at the mangled body and then glanced back at the naked figure lying nearby. "It was dark, you had no way of knowing there was anybody else," said the officer.

Just then, a dark sedan pulled up to the curb, and the detectives quickly emerged.

"We have two victims," explained the officer. "Apparently, they were attacked by some kind of animal."

The detectives paused for a moment, glanced down at the mangled body and the naked figure, and looked back at the man holding the gun. "You say it was an animal?" one of them asked.

The man nodded his head. "It was huge, something like a tiger."

"A tiger," murmured one of the detectives. "But we haven't had any reports of any animal escaping from any zoo."

"Well, it was some kind of animal," the man persisted. "It was growling and ripping apart that man over there. I fired a few shots and he disappeared into that alleyway."

They could hear the sound of the siren getting closer, screeching through the darkness, and then the flashing lights appeared and came bounding down the street.

"We found him lying in that alleyway," the officer who had argued with the naked man explained. "He said something about going back to his apartment and then fainted when he reached the street."

Two men in white uniforms, meanwhile, leaped from the halting ambulance and began examining the two bodies. They placed the mangled man on a stretcher and carried him toward the flashing lights.

"A tiger, you say?" one of the detectives repeated.

"He was right over there, big as life, with black stripes and hair all over his body—"

The men in white uniforms approached Kolak, still lying on the pavement, wrapped a white sheet over his lower body, and placed him on a stretcher. They halted for a moment when he suddenly raised his head and began to groan.

"But you don't understand," he said. "I can't go with you—"

He knew he couldn't explain why he couldn't go with them, but they would somehow have to understand.

One of the detectives, his gray-flecked hair gleaming in the glow of the streetlight, turned at the sound of the voice. He looked at the naked man's face, and stared into his eyes.

"You're Kolak, aren't you?" he finally said.

Kolak tried not to answer, decided he would remain silent, and then, he slowly nodded his head. They carried him off amid the red glare of the approaching dawn.

The tiger is roaring and then scampers into the darkness of the forest. Kolak's eyes close for a moment, and then suddenly he bolts upright, his body in the throes of a cold sweat. The beast has visited him once more, his mind and body totally subservient to the spirits hidden away in the darkness of the Malaysian forest. The *latah* . . .

"Mr. Kolak? Are you all right?"

Kolak stared up at the nurse, his body finally relaxing, the paralyzing trance fading from his mind. "I'll be fine," he whispered back.

"The detectives are here. They want to ask you a few questions. Are you feeling well enough to talk?"

"Send them in. I'm all right now."

She paused for a moment, glanced at the bandage enveloping his shoulder, and turned toward the door. "Don't worry, I won't let them stay very long," she said, walking away.

He followed her with his eyes as she opened the door and stepped outside. A few moments later, the door opened once again and two men in gray suits appeared.

"Hello, Mr. Kolak," one of them with graying hair said, walking toward him. "I hope you're feeling better. You gave us quite a scare. The name's Dempster."

"It's nothing serious," he replied.

"We just wanted to ask you a few questions. We wondered if you might be able to remember something about what happened."

"Not really. Everything seems to be shrouded in darkness."

"But you do remember that animal that attacked you, isn't that true? I believe it was described as a tiger."

"Yes, that's correct."

"But no tiger has escaped from anywhere, and certainly is not walking the streets of the city. Are you aware of that?"

"Then what are you saying, detective? Everyone was making it up or suffering from hallucinations?"

"To tell you the truth, Mr. Kolak, I don't know what to think. I mean there was definitely something that attacked those people, there's no doubt of that, but it doesn't seem to have been a tiger. So what we're wondering is, just what did attack those people, and yourself, I might add."

Kolak felt a sudden sharp pain in his shoulder and winced. "I thought it was a tiger," he finally replied.

"You thought it was a tiger, and so did everyone else who witnessed the attack, and yet, as I have said, there is no tiger." He halted, and stared into Kolak's eyes. "Maybe it was someone dressed as a tiger. You know, some sort of coat or something. A tiger skin, maybe. Is that possible?"

Kolak felt another sharp pain. "Yes I guess so," he grimaced.

"And yet, we have found no trace of this tiger coat anywhere. Only you lying naked in that alleyway with a bullet in your shoulder."

"What are you trying to say, detective?"

"Why did you show up at the crime scene on the morning of the first attack, Mr. Kolak?"

"I heard the disturbance, the noises, and thought I could be of some help."

"You heard the noises and thought they were being made by a tiger. Is that correct?"

"Yes, it sounded like a tiger."

"And you know something about tigers since you spent the last few months in Malaysia, isn't that true?"

"Well, the Malays worship the tiger. They say he commands certain animal spirits."

"And have you witnessed these spirits?"

Kolak winced once again and grabbed his aching shoulder. "I'm sorry, detective," he said. "But can we continue this at another time?"

"Yes, yes, sure we can," replied the detective. "You probably need some rest. We can continue when you're feeling better."

"That would be satisfactory," said Kolak.

Detective Dempster looked at his partner, and nodded him toward the door. They were about to leave when the graying detective glanced back at Kolak.

"I just wonder, Mr. Kolak, if you would be able to explain to me why there is a bullet in your shoulder when that man said he had fired at the beast, a beast, I might add, that probably does not exist."

"I don't know, detective, I just don't know," Kolak groaned. "Everything is just a blank, a void within my memory."

The detective frowned. "Well, we'll let you think about it," he finally said. "It'll probably come to you after sufficient rest." He then turned, motioned to the other detective, and they left the room.

Kolak placed his hand on his forehead, and wiped a few beads of sweat away. They had found him and there wasn't anything he could do about it. He sighed trying to calm himself down, and then began thinking of a way to stall for time. That's what he needed, *time*.

He watched as the door opened once again, and the nurse came back inside. "You're feeling pain, Mr. Kolak?" she asked.

He slowly nodded his head, holding his wounded shoulder.

"Well, these will put you to sleep for a while," she said, handing him a few pills and a glass of water. "There's plenty of time for them to bother you. You just get some rest."

He swallowed the pills, closed his eyes, and was soon drifting off to sleep.

There was laughter resounding through the air. One of the Malays, dark skinned with slightly wavy hair, was holding in his hands a long bamboo rod. Kolak watched as he blew into the bamboo, expelling a wooden dart from the other end. It struck a young boy, who immediately fell into a trance.

"He is of the *latah*," explained one of the men.

Then another man stepped forward. He was wearing a tiger skin, and his head was crowned by a band of bird feathers. There were tiger paws upon his feet. He carried a fur-covered drum, which he began beating with a wooden drumstick. The steady beat of the drum and the rising chant of the people soon brought on a frenzy of activity, and then the shaman stepped toward the young boy, who had drunk from the shaman's cup and was still in a hypnotic trance, and began conversing with the spirit taking possession of his soul.

The shaman then commanded the boy to rise to his feet, and he stood there snarling and growling like the beast of the forest under the midnight moon. Then the chickens were let loose, and the boy dropped to his knees and began chasing them while making the sounds of the cat. When he finally caught one of the chickens, he began devouring it as the cat, the beast, might do. The spirit of the tiger had entered his body, and he was no longer a boy, but a captive of the *latah* . . .

"Roger, Roger, please wake up."

Kolak opened his eyes, and could feel the sweat enveloping his face. He noticed the blonde female standing over him, and suddenly realized it was Gail.

"I-I was back in Malaysia," he stammered.

"It was all just a dream, darling," she replied, dabbing his forehead with a tissue. "You're still here in the hospital."

"But the shaman and the boy—"

"All just a nightmare, Roger. No one can hurt you here."

He propped himself up on the pillow and felt his shoulder. The pain had gone.

"The doctor said you are healing remarkably fast," she said, kissing him on the forehead. "Do you feel better now, my darling?"

He nodded, reached for her hand, and tried to smile. "You're too good to me, Gail," he said.

"I know, my darling, but why in heaven's name were you out there on the streets in the middle of the night, Roger?"

He looked at her, his attempt at a smile now slowly sagging into a grimace. "I really can't say—"

"But you must tell me."

"I tried to explain it to you. It was in Malaysia—"

"Oh, don't you see, Roger, the police are asking questions about you. They think you might be the one who murdered those people."

"I am the one, Gail—"

"Oh, please, Roger, don't talk like that. It's impossible for you to be a murderer. I know you too well. You're kind and sensitive, and well, I just won't believe it. But you must tell me what happened. It's the only way for me to help you."

"It is the *latah*, the curse placed upon me . . . the spirit of the tiger, the beast, entered my body, my soul . . ."

"Oh, nonsense, there isn't any curse, my darling. And what about the tiger? People say they saw him attacking those people. Oh, please, Roger, tell me you also saw him and rushed to help those people."

"I wish that I could," he replied, frowning.

"But you did see the tiger, isn't that true?"

He bowed his head. "Yes, Gail, I saw the tiger."

"Then you can tell them you were just trying to help those people . . . that you saw the tiger and knew what to do because you had been among them in Malaysia. Isn't that true, Roger?"

"Yes, I saw them in Malaysia—"

("He is of the latah . . .")

"That's what I thought. I knew you couldn't be a murderer."

He looked at her, stared into her eyes, deciding she must know, once and for all, what had happened to him. "I saw the tiger, Gail," he finally said.

"I knew it," she replied, tears rushing down her face. "But nobody knows where he went, Roger."

"That's because he's right here, right in front of you."

"Oh, Roger, what do you mean? I can't stand it anymore. You're talking in riddles and the police think you killed those people—"

"I did, Gail," he said, a tear running down his cheek. "You see *I* am the tiger."

3

THE DISEASE

DR. SHANKS SAT BEHIND A large wooden desk, a pair of round spectacles resting upon his aquiline nose. "An interesting case," he was saying. "Most interesting. You see Mr. Kolak actually believes he is the tiger."

Detective Dempster nodded his head. "Yes, that's what I figured. Did he tell you where he hid the tiger coat? We can't seem to find it."

"That's because there is no tiger coat, detective," replied the doctor. "You see Mr. Kolak believes he actually becomes the tiger, and his body takes the shape of the animal."

Dempster looked at his partner. "Are you telling me he transformed into that tiger?" he finally asked.

"No, detective, I did not say he was able to complete the transformation. That, of course, is impossible. I only said that he believed in his mind that he became this wild animal."

"But our eyewitnesses said he had stripes and hair all over him."

"It is but an hallucination brought on by mass hysteria and the very convincing actions of our friend, Mr. Kolak. You see Mr. Kolak suffers from a mental disorder we refer to as lycanthropy. You may have heard of it pertaining to the werewolf, the most well known of the transformations described, and yet, there have been cases from around the world in which the people involved take the form of the most dangerous wild animal of their particular region. For instance, in Scandinavia, it is the bear. It is generally wolves elsewhere in Europe and in northern Asia, jaguars in South America, the hyena or leopard in Africa, and the tiger in India, China, Japan, and elsewhere in Asia.

"You see these people actually believe they are victims of a supernatural condition in which they can transform into one of these animals," the doctor explained. "But we have found this belief to be a delusion, a part of a psychiatric disorder that is likely to occur among people who are susceptible to suggestion, or believe in reincarnation and the transmigration of souls."

"Then you're telling us our friend, Mr. Kolak, is a psycho, is that it, doctor?" The detective looked at his partner and smiled.

"I am saying that he suffers from this pathological condition," the doctor replied. "He is certainly not alone. Why, lycanthropy was even known to the Greeks and probably extended back into prehistoric times. Stories abounded of men frequenting cemeteries and living like dogs and wolves. The Romans called it, *versipellis*, or "turnskin." These stories of the werewolf spread throughout Europe during the Middle Ages and were widely believed. It is only recently we have come to identify it as a psychological disturbance."

"Then we can assume he'll be entering a plea of insanity?"

"I should think so," replied the doctor. "You see Mr. Kolak is a very sick man. I think that after we complete our observations, Mr. Kolak will be classified as suffering from delusions of persecution and grandeur combined with unrealistic, illogical thinking and hallucinations. I fear the onset of the disease was caused by a stressful experience in Mr. Kolak's life, Malaysia, I believe he said."

"Then you think he wanted to get caught, doctor?"

"Probably so. You see many who suffer from the disease desire to be treated before they experience the more severe and debilitating symptoms."

"I wondered why he showed up on the morning of the first attack," said the detective.

"I assume he was trying to give himself away."

"Well, he was so sure that it was a tiger, and yet, he had claimed he had not seen the attack or the creature. When we finally realized that there was no tiger, I began to suspect he was in some way connected to the murder."

"Yes, yes, he probably thought he was being suspected, anyway. You see someone suffering from paranoia will think or believe that other people are plotting against them or trying to harm, or persecute them in some way. Some trivial incident might have occurred in his life which he then began to exaggerate until he began to believe that you somehow knew he had been responsible for the murders."

"Well, I guess that explains it," said the detective. "He'll probably be assigned to you for a very long time."

"I imagine so. I am hopeful we can help Mr. Kolak. You see many patients suffering from the very same disease make a complete and permanent recovery."

"Yeah, and what about the victims, doctor?"

Dr. Shanks paused for a moment. "We do what we can, detective," he finally said. "At least, there is one life we can try to save."

Dempster nodded, turned to his partner, and motioned him toward the door. "We'll keep in touch, doctor," he said, opening the door.

"Very good, detective." He watched them leave the room and then spoke into his intercom. "Send Mr. Kolak in," he told the nurse.

A few minutes passed, and then the door opened once again. Kolak, pale and somber, stepped inside.

"Hello, Mr. Kolak," said the doctor. "Please be seated."

Kolak sat down in a chair positioned in front of the doctor's desk. "The detectives were here, weren't they?" he asked.

"You need not be concerned with them, Mr. Kolak. They won't be bothering you any longer. You see you'll be staying with us for a while."

"Oh, I understand. You've labeled me a nutcase—"

"Now, Mr. Kolak, no one here thinks of you as anything but a person with a problem. Besides, we don't use such harsh terms anymore. Modern medicine has come a long way over the years in dealing with such illnesses."

"And what illness would that be?"

"Well, I would say you have problems with paranoia and have even experienced hallucinations of some kind—"

("the latah . . .")

"Very good, doctor. You have placed me into one of your neat, little categories. I am honored. But your psychological generalizations can't explain what I suffer from."

"And what is that, Mr. Kolak?"

Kolak looked at him and frowned. "A curse, doctor," he finally said. "A curse that has subjugated my spirit causing me to be controlled by the will of the tiger. Is that in your little book of generalizations?"

The doctor stared at him, evaluating his words and bearing. "Why don't you tell me about the curse, Mr. Kolak?" he asked.

Kolak shifted in his chair. "I know you're not going to believe it, doctor, but it occurred over a period of time. There were sessions with the shaman—"

"Shaman?"

"A religious man who is believed to be able to heal the sick and to communicate with the world beyond."

"A witch doctor, Mr. Kolak?"

"If you prefer. Well, anyway, there are ceremonies in which he dresses in the skin of the tiger and beats his drum until the people begin to chant, and then the shaman is possessed by the spirit of the tiger."

"And he placed this spirit within you?"

"It's not so simple, doctor. There are salves and plant extracts and tiger skins and various rites in which the person is made to live like the tiger."

"Material aids to achieve hallucination. Yes, Mr. Kolak, and what were some of these rites?"

Kolak grimaced. "Many of them I don't remember. They placed me in a trance of some kind. But I do remember the sacrificial feast—" He paused for a moment. "You see we were supposed to live like the tiger, become the tiger, in every way, in every action."

"Yes, Mr. Kolak, and about the feast—"

"We were made to eat what the tiger would eat, what the man-eater would eat . . ."

"And that would be human flesh?"

Kolak looked down, a tear glistening in the light. "Human flesh was part of it," he said. "They mixed the human parts with meat and forced us to consume it, just like the animals we had become."

"And you came to believe you were the tiger?"

"Not only came to believe it, doctor, but actually transformed into the beast."

"Now, Mr. Kolak, you don't expect me to believe that you actually became this animal all because of some primitive voodoo—"

"Voodoo, doctor? Then how can you explain those people being mauled by a particularly ferocious animal? Do I look as if I'm capable of such violence? I tell you it's the curse, the *latah*."

He wondered why he was telling the doctor all this, and yet, he knew if there was any chance for the curse to be stopped, or prevented, he must try. *There were innocent lives at stake.*

"Nonsense, Mr. Kolak," the doctor continued. "It's nothing more than post-hypnotic suggestion that has become a psychological delusion aided by feelings of grandeur and persecution. Under such circumstances, you are capable of greater strength than you can imagine."

"So I'm forced to defend my very sanity now?"

"There's no need for that, Mr. Kolak. There are medications now that will be able to help you. Before you know it, you'll forget all about this ridiculous curse."

"But you don't understand, it's all true. We were forced to roll on the ground where the tiger had been, follow him on his hunting sprees and feed upon the dead carcasses . . . Don't you understand? We actually became the tiger. His spirit entered our bodies—"

"Nonsense, Mr. Kolak. These are the ways of hypnotic suggestion. You have been under a great stress, there's no doubt of that, but we can help you. Now, about those people who were murdered, did you realize what you were doing?"

Kolak looked down. "No, no, I don't seem to remember much when I go into the trance and become the tiger." He paused. "But I know what I have done. It all becomes very clear to me when I awake in the morning. The blood, the screams, they haunt my mind—"

"Very interesting," the doctor murmured. "You believe you have become the beast. That's why they found you naked in that alleyway."

"But I do become the beast, doctor. I am naked after my attacks because my clothing has split and shredded under the stress of the transformation. Don't you see? It's the *latah* . . ."

Dr. Shanks stared at him and began shaking his head. "Interesting," he said. "Very interesting."

"You'll never get out of here," laughed a man with a dent in his forehead as he watched Kolak walk across the room. "No one leaves here with any sense left in their head."

The man laughed once again, and then Kolak watched as he lit a cigarette and began puffing away in long, steady drags. "You're here for good, Kolak. You'd better get used to it."

As the man continued to laugh, he waved his burning cigarette in the air and then tossed it to the carpeting, stamping it out with his foot. "They say you killed two people, Kolak. You should be happy here, it's better than prison. That is, if you don't mind losing everything that's in your head. Well, it shouldn't matter to you. You probably want to forget. Ain't that right, Kolak?"

Kolak looked at him, deciding he didn't want to argue, especially since he was now trapped in the hospital psychiatric ward. He stared down at the many holes in the carpeting, remnants of lit cigarettes carelessly flung down due to apathy or madness.

"Got a girlfriend, Kolak?" asked the man with a sneering grin. "I bet she doesn't mind you being dragged off into oblivion. She probably has a lot of boys just waiting to get into her panties and make her scream. Don't you think so, Kolak?"

He listened to the man's laughter, echoing through his brain, as the thought of Gail gnawed at his very soul. "Why don't you mind your own business, you crazy bastard," he finally said.

The man leaned forward, spittle hanging from his lips. "I may be a crazy bastard, Kolak, but she's probably already had her fair share of the boys by now!"

Kolak's face contorted with anger as he lunged for the man's throat. The man gasped, and could feel the hands clutching with deadly intent. Kolak looked down at the man with scorn, a blind fury coursing through his body, and then in the midst of this murderous clench, he felt powerful hands rip him from his victim and fling him backwards to the wall.

He could hear the man gasping for breath, the feet of the attendants shuffling across the floor. Then one of the men hit him in the stomach, and Kolak slumped forward and crashed to the carpet below. After a few minutes, he could hear the voices of nurses and doctors shouting in the hallway as one of the attendants sat on top of him hitting him in the head.

"That's enough, bring him to the quiet room," ordered one of the nurses from behind.

Kolak, meanwhile, could feel the hate surging within him, the snarl of the beast resounding through his mind. It was the curse, the *latah*. He then fell into a seizure, and began writhing on the floor.

"We will have to sedate him," said one of the doctors. "Get him to the quiet room."

Kolak could feel the beast emerging. He clenched his teeth and his hands, beads of sweat forming on his forehead, and then, everything was suddenly swallowed by darkness . . .

He could see the tiger stepping through the high grass, spotting a lamb in the distance. He watched as it walked slowly toward its intended victim, following its every action as it steadily approached. Then suddenly the tiger began to run toward the helpless prey. There was the anticipation of the tasting of blood, the tearing of flesh, when there was a sudden noise, a snapping of metal, and the realization that it had been caught in a trap . . .

Kolak opened his eyes and sat up, realizing he had been placed in a small room with no windows. This was the quiet room, where patients who displayed any kind of aggression were taken. He stood up, staring at the tangled shadows projected on the wall, wondering why he hadn't changed into the beast. His clothes were not torn, there was no blood trickling from his mouth, no screams echoing through his mind. Somehow, they had prevented the spirit of the tiger from entering his body.

He heard the lock snap, and the door swing open. Dr. Shanks was standing in the light.

"So I see you are still a man," said the doctor.

"How did you do it?" questioned Kolak. "How did you prevent the tiger from entering me?"

"I see you are not so pleased with our modern medications. I do not think the shaman knows anything about chlorpromazine or haloperidol. Is that not true, Mr. Kolak?"

"But the *latah* is strong—"

"Stronger than modern medicine? I think not, Mr. Kolak. You see you are making great strides to a full and complete recovery just as I said you would. Now why don't you come out of that room so that we can get rid of that ridiculous curse, once and for all."

Kolak took a few steps into the light and gazed down the corridor. "Then I'm stuck here for a very long time, is that not true, doctor?" he said.

"We will see, Mr. Kolak. There is still that matter of killing two people. You realize if your recovery is too quick, you will be placed inside a prison cell, anyway. Either way, I don't expect that you will be a free man for quite a while."

Kolak looked at him and stepped forward. He glanced at the nurse's station, where the medications were being prepared, and walked toward the television room, wondering if the curse had really been broken.

"I told you you'd never get out of here, Kolak," said the man with the dent in his forehead as he sat on the couch smoking a cigarette. "Do you think the doctors here believe any of your crazy stories?"

Kolak sat down on a nearby chair. "You're lucky they don't, Jankers, my friend, or you would have been dead last night."

Jankers flicked the cigarette to the floor and laughed. "I knew you couldn't kill me, Kolak, not with all the security in this place. And even if you had, you would have been doing me a favor."

Kolak looked at him and grimaced. "I just don't understand it," he finally said. "I should have changed into the tiger last night."

"You and me both," said Jankers, spitting on the carpeting.

"No, you don't understand, I become the tiger and then kill—"

Jankers began to laugh. "Now you trying one of your crazy stories on me, Kolak? Well, I may be crazy, but I ain't stupid. A tiger yet. Ain't it supposed to be a wolf howling at the moon?"

"I should have killed you last night."

As Jankers laughed, Kolak stood up and walked out of the television room. Although part of him was relieved the tiger did not materialize, he had hoped the curse would somehow help him to escape or get him killed, thereby ending his misery forever.

He walked down one of the corridors, and could see an attendant leaving through the locked front door. For some reason, the door didn't seem to close properly, didn't seem to lock with the customary click. He slowly shuffled toward the door, trying not to attract any attention, and placed his hand on the knob. He pushed slightly and the door opened.

He stepped into the hallway, and rushed toward one of the adjoining corridors. If he could just avoid detection, he would be far away before they even noticed he had gone.

He put his head down and walked calmly down the corridor. Spotting a doctor, he turned around and headed back from where he had come. He was about to make his way down the main corridor, hoping he wouldn't be recognized, when he heard a voice from behind.

"Don't you think you should inform us before you leave, Mr. Kolak?" said the voice.

He spun around and stared into the face of Dr. Shanks. Kolak gasped with surprise, and then in a moment of panic, dashed down the corridor. He could hear Dr. Shanks summoning the attendants from behind. If he could only make it to the front door and somehow get outside, he would have a chance . . .

Weaving his way through the startled people, he spotted the front entrance of the hospital. The glass doors gleamed in the glistening sun. He could hear the hurried footsteps behind him, and knew the attendants were coming. Kolak dashed toward the front doors, glimpsing the trees and their canopy of leaves swaying in the wafting breeze. He was almost there . . . almost free . . .

Kolak lunged for the front doors when he was suddenly tackled from behind. He fell to the floor, and then was pounced upon by several attendants. As he struggled with his captors, another seizure overcame him. The attendants watched as he wriggled beneath them, his teeth in a vicious clench. After a few moments, Kolak stopped moving. He had lost consciousness, and Dr. Shanks ordered the attendants to pick him up and carry him back to the psychiatric ward.

4

THE TRANSFORMATION

THEY SAT IN A CIRCLE, each patient recounting their attempts at suicide, when Dr. Shanks looked at Kolak.

"Mr. Kolak, have you ever tried to take your own life?" he asked.

Kolak looked down. Ever since his attempted escape and his eventual return to the mental ward, he had become lethargic, uninterested in food or activity. Dr. Shanks had noticed this, too, with some satisfaction, for he knew it meant Kolak had become just another individual beaten by the system, a system that encouraged conformity and submission.

"No, I never . . ." stammered Kolak. "But recently I've had thoughts of doing myself in."

"Excellent," replied Dr. Shanks. "It's definitely a sign of health, Mr. Kolak, when you can objectively evaluate your particular situation."

"But I never wanted to kill myself before," he said, placing his head in his hands. "There was always Gail and my career as an anthropologist—"

"And all of that is gone now, isn't it, Mr. Kolak? No longer can you depend on anything that used to give you comfort and security. You're alone now without any hope. Very good, it's no wonder you've been thinking about taking your own life. A very healthy sign."

Kolak moaned.

"Now what about you, Jankers?" asked the doctor.

The man with the dent in his forehead leaned forward. "Many times," he replied enthusiastically. "Geez, there isn't a day that goes by when I don't think about snuffing myself—"

"This is absurd," interrupted Kolak, a renewed intensity pulsing through his system.

Dr. Shanks looked at him and frowned. "You've had your turn to speak, Mr. Kolak. I think we should allow Mr. Jankers to continue."

"But these sessions are ludicrous," Kolak argued. "Why do you expect us to sit here and tell you about how we tried to knock ourselves off?"

"Because, Mr. Kolak, it is imperative that we grasp reality and evaluate ourselves as we really are and not as we would like to be."

"You asshole!"

Kolak leaped from his chair and onto Dr. Shanks, who shuddered with fear. "I'll show you what snuffing it is all about, doctor," he shouted, as his hands clutched the doctor's throat.

As Kolak shook the doctor's head, several attendants came rushing into the room. They grabbed Kolak, and after a fierce struggle, they tore him from the doctor and threw him to the floor.

The other patients laughed and applauded as they watched the doctor lean back in his chair, fighting for breath. When he had finally stopped choking, he looked down at Kolak and sneered.

"Obviously your therapy is not working, Mr. Kolak," said the doctor. "I think I will recommend you for electroconvulsive treatment. Then maybe you won't be so quick to attack your fellow human beings."

Kolak gritted his teeth and tried to lunge for the doctor. The attendants grabbed him and pulled him back to the floor.

"Yes, that's right, Mr. Kolak, get angry," said the doctor. "Angry enough to pull me apart, just as you did to those people you murdered. Do you feel the tiger inside you, Kolak? Yes, yes, let him emerge. I want to see what that witch doctor put inside you!"

Kolak clenched his teeth, his body writhing in anger. As the attendants held him down, he went into a convulsive fit.

"Is this the transformation, Kolak?" shouted the doctor. "Have you become the tiger? Yes, yes, Kolak, hate me. Hate me with all your soul.

You're going to be here for a very long time. Until there is nothing left of you, except those pitiful memories—"

Kolak opened his mouth and screamed, although to those around him it sounded like a deep and haunting glissando. The attendants looked down and could see his face thicken, broaden to a wide oval, then almost melt away before their eyes. They watched the continual swift distortions with rapt trepidation, and then noticed his clothes were stretching, bulging at the seams and then splitting into ragged shreds of cloth. His eyes, meanwhile, had turned a glistening yellow, and fangs began to emerge from the corners of his mouth. The attendants watched this rapid transformation, the hair sprouting wildly across his forehead and from the sides of his face, and finally jumped up and pedaled backwards to the door.

Dr. Shanks stood and stared at the beast, whose back was arched, his arms and legs still growing, covered with a reddish tan fur with black stripes, as he arose from the floor and snarled. The patients in the room, meanwhile, leaped out of their chairs and scrambled backwards, their minds trying to decide whether this was reality or some wild psychotic episode.

"What evil lies within a man's soul?" cried the doctor. "What beast hides within the human mind?"

The beast growled, and then spread his fingers, allowing long, sharp claws to burst from the nails. He glanced at Dr. Shanks, still standing in front of him unable to move, opened his mouth, and bit down across the doctor's face.

The doctor screamed in horror as the blood dripped from his chin, his face a mass of mangled flesh. Then the beast sunk his claws into his body, and ripped the beating heart from his chest. The doctor watched in shock and disbelief as the beast ate his heart, and then, with a quizzical look on his bloodied face, Dr. Shanks collapsed in a heap upon the floor.

The beast snarled, and then striding on its hind legs, watched as the attendants ripped open the door and rushed from the room screaming. The beast followed them, leaping upon one of the attendants and tearing open his throat. Blood spilled wildly across the floor as the beast ripped a chunk of flesh from the body and then moved back toward the windows. Amid a commotion of screaming and shouting and fleeing human bodies, the beast grabbed one of the window gratings and tore it from its place. There were more shrieks of horror as security guards dashed down the corridors, wielding pistols and poised to fire.

The beast paused for a moment, snarled, and then glimpsed the guards racing toward him. Before a shot could be fired, there was the shattering of glass as the beast leaped through the window. He landed on the ground, still snarling, and bounded toward the nearby trees.

Shots echoed through the mist of twilight as the beast hurried away. He finally disappeared amid the shadows and the fading light.

"Did you get him?" asked one of the doctors, still finding it hard to believe what his eyes had seen.

"Don't think so," replied one of the guards, peering through the smashed window. "But it's getting dark. It's hard to tell."

"What the hell was it?" asked one of the stunned nurses, her body still quivering with fear.

"A delusion come true," said the doctor.

As the night deepened, isolated screams could be heard across the landscape, swelling into a great paroxysm of fear. The beast was headed northward, away from the glare of the lights and the clamor and clatter of a city well accustomed to the unusual. He was headed into the darkness, free to stalk the night, and the thought of such a notion caused a shiver to run down the spine of even the most dispassionate.

Kolak hurried through the shadows, grunting his disdain. He was free again, and as he rushed through the lattice of moonlight and shadow, he vowed to himself he would never be captured again. If they still wanted him, they would have to fight him to the death.

He glanced down at his arms, covered in thick, matted hair, and knew he was one with the beast once more. It was as if he was drifting through a dream, fully conscious, and yet, not able to fully control his actions. He had read about hallucination and the drugs used that induced such episodes. There were henbane and nightshade, both used in medieval times to induce illusions, and extensively utilized in witchcraft. There was also a rye grain fungus called, ergot, which was known to produce a compound similar to LSD and cause hallucinatory sensations very much like physical transformation.

He had read about all these substances, had even sampled them among the Malays, and still there was no way to explain how a man could actually change into the beast. But it had occurred. There was no doubt of that.

He kept rushing through the darkness, trying to think of where to go, fighting against the murderous impulse that raced through his mind and body, and then suddenly tripped over something and fell hard to the ground. He growled, looked down, and noticed it was a stone of some kind. There were words scrawled on top of it, and then Kolak turned his head and could see amid the yellow tinge that pervaded his vision, numerous high, rounded stones covering the landscape. *Tombstones.*

He realized he had somehow stumbled into a cemetery, and the thought seemed to comfort him in some strange way. Here was death all around him, he could feel it in the air, and somehow, there was a feeling of tranquility, of serenity. He rested for a moment, grumbled with some satisfaction, and then stood up and gazed at the rows of tombstones.

Death. The thought floated through the midnight sky. He began to wonder if that was the only thing that could really free him from the curse. Death. But was he prepared to relinquish his life for some form of possible peacefulness? He thought for a moment, then sneered, his lips quivering, and dismissed the notion. There was still a chance he would be able to find the cure, the way to finally prevent it from occurring again, and there was still Gail to think about. No, he wasn't prepared to die just yet. He would struggle on, while there was still a chance . . .

He could see the tiger snarl, bare his fangs, and slowly step through the dark shadows. He then heard a sound, a crackling of a twig, the brushing of leaves, and followed it into the glowing moonlight. There was life and death in the air, it filled his senses, and the murderous urge coursing through his veins drove him onward into the night . . .

Kolak opened his eyes, and realized he was back in the city, the tombstones having transformed once again into the towering buildings that huddled amid the bright glaze of city light. This was a cemetery of a different kind, and he knew if he wanted to stay alive, he would have to find a way out from among the buildings. He would head north, search for the open land that stretched beyond the twinkling lights of the distant bridge. There, he would be able to roam free, and have plenty of time to think. *Time,* that's what he needed. *Time to think.*

He disappeared into a nearby alleyway, and then heard voices in the shadows and the darkness. They were voices of men drinking, the bottles clinking against the dirty cement. He approached slowly, trying to remain as quiet as possible, and listened to their words. As he listened, he bared his fangs, the saliva dripping down and bathing his torn shirt in the juices of anticipation . . .

"I tell you, there's evil everywhere these days," slurred one of the men, who was holding a bottle in one of his hands. "Why, it's a wonder all of the buildings don't come crashing down."

"The end is coming soon, there's no doubt of that," replied one of the others. "Just as the good book says."

The other man slurped at the bottle, wiped his lips on his ragged sleeve, and then passed the bottle to the next man. He gurgled for a moment, sighed, and then passed it to the third man.

"Geez, this is good booze," the second man said. "Now all we need are some horny chicks—"

The two other men laughed at the statement, and then they began passing the bottle around once again . . .

Kolak watched as the three men took turns drinking from the bottle. He snarled for a moment, and then suppressed the urge to snarl again. This would be a rather easy kill, he assured himself. He could hear another voice inside him, faint and distant, attempting to warn him about the possible consequences of another attack, disregarded it, and slowly advanced toward the three delinquents.

He could see they were so busy drinking and laughing, they didn't even notice as he crept up behind them . . .

"None for me?"

A hoarse, snarling voice shot through the air, and before they could even react, a huge beast that looked something like a tiger standing on his hind legs appeared beside them.

"What the hell?" gasped one of the men.

There was a shattering of glass as the bottle fell to the ground and exploded into a million shards. Then the growl of the beast thundered through the air, and before another moment passed, one of the men felt the sting of something sharp across his face.

The other two men stared at the gouged cuts running down the man's face and began to tremble in fear and disbelief. Then the beast roared and one of the men slumped to the ground with a huge slash across his neck, the blood pouring out between his grasping fingers.

The third man, staring at the blood and torn flesh, tried to run, but the alcohol had already flooded his mind and body. As he attempted to flee, his legs tangled, his feet stumbled, and he promptly fell to the pavement. He watched in horror, as if he was in the midst of some terrible nightmare, the thrashings of his two companions as they finally succumbed to the attacks and limply slid to the cement in bloody, mangled heaps.

As drunk as he was, the instinct to remain still and hope the fiend would disregard him flashed through his brain. He closed his eyes, and still shaking, placed his head on the pavement. A few moments elapsed, and then attempting to determine whether the beast had gone, he slowly opened one of his eyes . . .

The first thing he saw was the feet of the beast beside him. He heard a growl, the slash of the claws through the air, and then felt the rivulets of blood streaming down his face . . .

Kolak stepped back from the kill and let out a fierce snarl. There was nothing he could do to stop the beast, but he knew if he wanted to save himself he would have to attempt to leave the city. He would go north, toward the lights of the bridge, and then make his way across and flee into the nearby wooded banks of the Hudson . . .

He dashed from the alleyway, into the glow of the streetlight, and headed toward the bridge. He kept running, trying to stay hidden as much as possible among the shadows and the darkness. Every so often, he felt as if someone was following him, but in the state of the beast there was nothing he could do about it and hurried onward . . .

Kolak continued to run through the darkened streets, and soon he could see the bridge and its sparkling lights hovering before him. He staggered forward, fell to one knee, and he knew the transformation was beginning to fade. As he felt his body begin to contract, melt back into the human being he was born to be, he wondered whether death was the only way he could prevent the changes from occurring once again. *Death* . . .

He had enough of the hallucinations, the transformations, and the killing. What had begun as a curiosity, a study of the human soul, had become a great burden, one he could no longer endure by himself. The thought of leaping off the bridge into the icy waters below flitted through his mind, and then before he could contemplate it any further, he felt the steady glare of headlights upon him and dashed away. They were following him was the thought that rushed through his brain. They had come to take him back, back to where there were no tomorrows, no hope of escaping the past . . .

Kolak felt his legs churning, the sound of his feet tapping the cement pervading the air. He rushed through the blinding lights, finally staggered off the bridge, and hurried down the intersecting highway ramp . . .

He was free now, he had made it to the other side, but before he could reach the nearby trees, he felt his knees weaken and his arms go limp. He faltered for a moment, and then toppled beside the highway into a slumbering heap.

5

THE COVEN

KOLAK OPENED HIS EYES AND stared up into the growing daylight. He was lying in the grass, by the side of a highway, half-naked with blood spilling down from his mouth across his bare chest.

"Are you all right, mister?" a man was shouting over him.

He looked up, could see a tall, burly man standing there in a plaid shirt and jeans.

"Where am I?" he muttered.

"Why, you're on the other side of the bridge," the man replied. "Where do you live?"

Kolak closed his eyes, did not know what to say, and groaned.

"Are you hurt?" the man asked.

"I'll be all right," he finally said, getting to his feet. He stared up at the man, realizing he was almost seven feet tall.

"If you've got no place to go, or if you're running away from somewhere, I'd be more than happy to take you back to my place until you get settled," said the man. "It looks to me as if you're in no condition to go anywhere, anyway, at the present time."

"You have no idea what happened to me last night?" asked Kolak, somewhat suspicious of the man's true intentions.

"I don't know what you mean, mister," replied the man. "I was driving along and saw you lying there. I thought you might need some help. Why don't you come back with me? I'll help fix you up good as new."

Kolak nodded and followed the man back to his car, a black sedan which looked much like a car used by the detectives. "You work for the police department?" he finally asked, trying to stay calm.

"Are you kidding?" replied the man. "That's pretty funny. That's probably the last profession I would ever be associated with."

The man's reply seemed to satisfy him, so he opened the door and climbed inside. He watched as the man bent down, and leaned back in the driver's seat, which had been positioned away from the steering wheel, almost touching the back seat.

"The name's Charlie Endor," he said, placing the key in the ignition. "My place is about an hour north of here. You going to be all right?"

"Yeah, I guess so," Kolak replied. "I was just wondering if you'd stop somewhere so I can get cleaned up."

"Sure, no problem. I'll stop at the next gas station. How's that?"

"That would be fine, but aren't you wondering where all this blood came from?"

Endor smiled. "Well, I was a little curious," he said. "Are you in any kind of trouble?"

Kolak paused for a moment. "Everything's all right now, Mr. Endor. I was in some kind of fight last night, although I really don't remember it very well," he said.

Endor looked at him and smiled once again. "Well, here's the gas station," he said. "I have a shirt on the back seat. You take it and put it on after you get washed up."

Kolak nodded, retrieved the shirt, and made his way to the bathroom. After several moments, he reappeared looking somewhat revitalized. "I can't thank you enough, mister," he said, upon sliding back into the car. "I don't know what I would have done without you. My name's Kolak, Roger Kolak."

"Glad to meet you, Mr. Kolak. It's good that you're feeling better."

"Well, what brought you to the city, anyway?" asked Kolak. "Considering you live in the suburbs."

Endor paused, and turned his head. "Why, you did, Mr. Kolak," he said.

"Me? Why, have we met before?"

"No, Mr. Kolak, we haven't, but I have heard about you."

"You interested in anthropology?"

"No, I'm interested in you, Mr. Kolak—"

Kolak stared down at his hands, trying to remain calm. "And why is that?" he finally asked.

"Because I know who and what you are, Mr. Kolak."

Kolak began searching for the door lock, thoughts of leaping from the car flitting through his mind. "I-I don't know what you mean," he stammered.

"Relax, Mr. Kolak. "We are people who understand."

"What do you mean?"

"Oh, come on, Kolak, the transformation. How do you think I spotted you this morning? I saw you roaming the streets last night and followed you over the bridge."

"But how could you know?"

"I told you, we understand. We're people like you and want to help you attain command over your special powers."

"Then you're not with the police department or the hospital?"

"No, no, Mr. Kolak. Wait and you'll see."

"Then you know I become the beast?"

Endor looked over and smiled. "It's the reason we've been looking for you."

Kolak sat and stared out the window, wondering just who these people were. He hoped they weren't part of some crazy cult enamored with his ability to change into some raging beast. He thought of trying to get away, of making him stop the car with some excuse and then run, but decided to wait.

Time passed, and soon Endor pulled off the highway. He finally came to a halt in front of an old Victorian house, painted dark brown, with a porch running across the front entrance and wrapping around both sides.

"This is it," said Endor, turning off the motor. "Why don't you come inside?"

Kolak nodded, resigned to finding out who these people were, and followed Endor to the front door. Endor knocked several times until the door slowly opened, and a female with black hair in a long, purple robe was standing in the dark opening.

"Hello, Jessie," Endor said. "This is Mr. Kolak."

"Come in," she said in a whisper. "We've been waiting for you."

They stepped inside, walked down a narrow hallway, and came to a large room lit only by several candles. Kolak stared down at the pentagram etched in the middle of the floor, something that looked like an altar nearby, and a collection of nine-inch daggers on the opposite wall.

"What is this place?" he whispered.

"It's called a coven, Mr. Kolak," replied Endor, the pale, haunting light of the candles shimmering across his body.

"Then you are all witches?" asked Kolak.

"That's correct, Mr. Kolak, although these days we prefer the term, Wiccans."

"And you engage in black magic?"

"If you prefer, Mr. Kolak. You see each one of us specializes in a particular branch of magic. Most of us have used black, as well as white witchcraft, to achieve our objectives."

"Then you'd be able to put an end to this curse I suffer from?"

"If that's your preference," replied Endor. "But we were hoping you'd come to accept this thing you refer to as a curse, and learn how to use it to your advantage."

He watched as several men and women entered the room, and soon counted eleven.

"How many people are in this coven?" Kolak asked.

"There are the eleven you see here," said Endor. "You are the twelfth."

"And what about you?"

"I am the leader or devil, if you prefer. You see Mr. Kolak today is Roodmas, one of the assemblies or Sabbaths that take place during the year."

He stared at the other people in the room, male and female, black and white, all wearing the long purple robes, and wondered whether he wanted to remain here as one of their members. He then decided if he was ever to rid himself of the curse, it would be advantageous to learn the ways of magic.

"Please follow me, Mr. Kolak, we were waiting for you to join us before we began the celebrations," Endor said. "Everybody here knows who and what you are, so there should be no problem with fitting in. We have great respect for you, Mr. Kolak. I think you should know that."

One of the females stepped forward and handed Kolak a robe. "Please put this on, Mr. Kolak," she said. "I am Charlie's wife, Lil. I am most pleased that you decided to join us."

Kolak put on the robe and watched as the others began carrying food out to the adjoining room. "We begin with a feast," said Endor. "I hope you're hungry, despite last night's activities."

The feast . . . the plates of meat mixed with human arms, fingers, and entrails being placed upon the table. The shaman chanting as they were forced to take the human flesh and eat it while praising the tiger spirits. Once one ate of the human flesh, the legend went, one could not become a man again unless he abstained from flesh for nine years. Nine years. He remembered the ritual dances, the Malays writhing to the drumbeat, entreating the spirits to enter their bodies. The tiger moving quietly through the forest, leaving sacrificial remains behind which they were forced to devour to strengthen the bond between man and beast. The *latah* . . .

Kolak watched as the members of the coven began to dance, some of them leaping over candle flames placed upon the pentagram. They began to chant the name of their god, and Kolak felt the beads of sweat forming on his forehead. He then fell to the floor, writhing uncontrollably in a spasmodic fit . . .

"*Try to control it, Kolak.*" He could hear Charlie Endor's voice flitting through his brain. *Try to control it.*

Kolak felt himself falling into the trance, when suddenly he was lifted to his feet from behind. He looked up at Endor and frowned.

"You must try to control it, Kolak," Endor said. "And use it to your advantage."

Kolak stared at him. "You don't understand, do you?" he replied. "I am becoming the beast again."

He then turned, ran down the narrow hallway, opened the door, and hurried outside into the misty twilight.

Detective Dempster marched down the hallway, knocked at the door, and stepped inside.

"Have you found him?" asked the silver-haired doctor from behind the desk.

The detective shook his head and grimaced. "I still find it hard to believe," he finally said.

"Well, Detective Dempster, you can be sure we witnessed it ourselves before we had the audacity to tell you about it," replied the doctor. "After all, in our profession, this is totally inconsistent with the dictates of reality. In fact, had there not been doctors and nurses to see the actual event, it would have undoubtedly been classified as a mass delusion. Besides, we have the bodies to prove it."

"But an actual transformation—"

"It's a pathological condition, detective, one that is classified as extremely rare. You see psychological delusion is the more common form of the disease, but pathological lycanthropes do exist. They were once very common in medieval Europe, but medicine has come a long way since then. I believe those affected by the disease would flee to the woods and mangle their victims at night."

"Well, police work has come a long way since then also, Dr. Keld."

"Indeed. I believe quite a few supposed werewolves were, in fact, apprehended back in the fifteen and sixteen hundreds, detective. According to my research, Pierre Burgot, Michel Verdun, Gilles Garnier, and oh yes, a Peter Stumpf were placed on trial and actually executed by French and German courts. There are also the cases of a man named Roulet, who was tried in 1598, and of Jean Grenier in 1603, who was subsequently convicted and pronounced insane. The Roulet case is particularly interesting in that he was thought to be a 'wolf child,' that is, raised by wolves."

"According to Dr. Shanks, Kolak believed he was placed under some sort of spell—"

"Yes, yes, quite like the explanation given by Jean Grenier, who said he had been made a lycanthropist by a supernatural being he had met in the forest, and similar to the accounts given by wereleopards in India. According to Dr. Shanks' notes, Kolak fell into a trance caused by a Malaysian shaman. Apparently, this state of extreme suggestion is known as the *latah*."

"Is there any way to break the spell?"

"It must be done by a shaman. In the patient's condition, it is the only figure he believes has the power to lift the spell."

The detective frowned. "Do you know where we might find one of these shamans?"

"Well, I think you would have to look in Asia, although it is said they can be found in North and South America, southeastern India, Australia, and in other parts of the world. It comes from a Manchu-Tungus word meaning 'he who knows.'"

"Well, maybe we should find one of these shamans—"

"You realize, of course, it's all part of primitive superstition, wholly irrational based upon ignorance and a fear of the unknown."

"Yes, but if Kolak believes it, there's a chance we can capture him."

"I suppose," said the doctor, "we are compelled to do everything possible to put an end to the killing."

"That's what we intend to do, doctor. It's the reason why I brought the girl."

"You mean his girlfriend?"

The detective nodded. "Yes, Gail Hearn. She agreed to help us find Kolak."

"Very good. She has been most helpful already I understand. Dr. Shanks was quite appreciative of her willingness to cooperate. Tell her to come in."

The detective opened the door and stepped outside. A few moments later, the striking blonde woman entered the room, followed by the detective.

"Hello, doctor," she said somberly. "I'm so sorry all of this could not be prevented. You see, I refused to believe Roger was capable of killing anyone."

"Then he was completely normal before he made that trip to Malaysia?" asked the doctor.

"Roger was a kind, caring soul who would not think twice about helping a complete stranger," she replied. "I loved him very much and had planned to marry him as soon as he returned."

"Very interesting," said the doctor. "Then maybe he's not a lost cause, my dear. Maybe there is still some good inside him. We can only hope."

"If only I could talk to him," she said. "Tell him that he must turn himself in before he kills again. That there is a chance he can be treated, cured, of this terrible disease."

"I am hoping the same thing," replied the doctor. "If he only believed there was a way to help him."

"But he only believes in that curse, doctor. The *latah*, he called it. He said the tiger's spirit entered his body."

"I know, I know," the doctor said with a wave of his hand. "He told Dr. Shanks all about the curse. It's in his notes. He believes it was placed upon him by a shaman, a witch doctor."

"Yes, he mentioned the shaman."

"Do you have any idea where he is now?" asked the detective with a frown.

"As I told you, he has not tried to contact me after his escape from the hospital. God only knows where he might be."

"Well, wherever he is, those nearby are certainly not safe once darkness falls," said the detective.

He looked at her, and she bowed her head, trying to hold back the tears.

6

HUMAN FLESH

"MR. KOLAK!"

Charlie Endor hurried toward a clump of trees amid the growing darkness, a cooling breeze rushing in from the north. Peering between the trees, he could hear the shuffling of footsteps from behind the bushes.

"Mr. Kolak?"

He could hear the rustling of leaves and an odd snarling drifting through the air.

"Get away from here, Charlie!"

Kolak's voice soared into the shifting wind.

"But you must learn how to control it, Kolak," Endor replied. "You see, then it wouldn't be a curse anymore, but a blessing that could be used to your advantage."

"You don't know what you're talking about, Charlie. You know nothing about what's happening to me. Get away from here before you get hurt. I'm not responsible for what I might do once I become the beast."

Endor took a few steps forward, squinting into the darkness. "But you must listen, Roger. You can't afford to be so reckless with such power—"

"How would you know?"

Endor sighed, stepped forward, and pulled back the branches of the bush. "I guess I have no choice but to show you," he said.

Kolak stared at him, still in the midst of transformation. Hair was sprouting across his forehead as he watched Endor's head and spine suddenly slide up into the air, dangle for a moment, and then straighten once again as his chest bulged against the seams of his shirt. As the shirt burst open, Endor's head began to change, elongate. In moments, his whole body was distorting, growing, until the beast finally emerged.

Kolak stared up at the ten-foot bear-like creature before him. Endor snarled as Kolak turned and dashed away into the darkness. The last thing he wanted was to expend energy fighting a creature like himself, especially since he knew it would be Charlie Endor he would be fighting.

He raced through the bushes, his own face beginning to melt into the visage of the tiger, and hurried away. The spirit of the tiger had now enveloped his mind and body, and the only thing he desired was to hunt for human flesh . . .

He could see the tiger moving slowly through the darkness, stalking his prey, waiting for the chance to strike and taste the blood that would sustain him through the heat of the afternoon. He heard the voices of his prey in the distance, drawing him onward, pulling him ever closer. He approached silently, cautiously, readying himself for the attack . . .

"Put the car in the garage, Carolyn." Bill Evers stared up into the dark sky. "Don't want to give anyone any kind of temptation," he said.

His wife frowned. "You and your suspicions," she replied, fishing for the keys in her handbag. "Nobody ever comes around here."

"Better to be safe than sorry, and it's a good thing they don't. Why, the last thing we need is a lot of people nosing around in our affairs."

"Like they'd find anything of interest," Carolyn said, pushing the key inside the door lock. "Honestly, you must be the most suspicious man in the entire world."

"Better safe than sorry," Evers muttered back. He watched as his wife started the engine, sending great puffs of gray smoke sputtering into the air. As she slowly pulled the car forward, Evers thought he saw something in the corner of his eye; some sort of black shadow moving among the bushes. He turned his head and peered into the darkness. A warm wind flitted among the leaves and branches. He frowned, turned back toward the house, and watched as the car slowly rolled inside the garage.

A moment later, he thought he heard something moving among the trees. He looked over toward the shadows, shifting in the rushing wind, and frowned once again.

"What's wrong now?" His wife's voice startled him, and as he turned his head, he choked back the desire to gasp.

"Thought I heard something," he replied.

"You and your suspicions," she hissed with a frown. "Nobody ever comes around here."

As he watched her turn and hurry into the house, he grimaced. Then he turned his head and stared once again into the darkness. There was no movement except for the bending of the tree branches in the strong breeze. Shaking his head, he stepped into the opened garage.

"Did you find the bogey man?" his wife asked as he entered the house.

"Nothing there," he replied. "I guess it was just the wind."

"What a shame," she said sarcastically. "I thought maybe we finally had some company."

He frowned, walked to the living room, sat down, and grabbed the newspaper.

"Maybe if you weren't so suspicious, somebody might have the courage to stop by," he could hear his wife saying. "Honestly, you don't trust anybody, do you?"

He held the newspaper, still frowning, and glanced at a story about one of the local politicians. He began reading, trying to forget his wife's comments, when a sudden scream echoed from the kitchen.

Evers jumped up, threw down the newspaper, and rushed toward his wife, who was standing in the middle of the kitchen sobbing.

"What the hell happened?" he asked with concern.

"I-I saw it," his wife stammered. "Staring through the window—"

"Saw what?"

"The bogey man!" she shouted.

"Now, now, calm down, dear. It was just your imagination."

"B-But you said you thought you heard something. Well, I just saw what it was—"

"Now, come on, you never believe me. You think I'm always being suspicious."

She looked at him, sighed, and began walking toward the telephone.

"What are you doing now?" he asked.

"Why, I'm calling the police, that's what I'm doing," she replied. "Honestly, you said yourself there was something out there."

"But I didn't see anything—"

"But I did."

"I just don't think we should go bothering the police until we know for sure that something is out there."

"What do you propose?"

"Well, I think I should have a look around first," he said.

"But that thing is out there. You'll be killed."

"Now, now, I just want to be sure."

"You and your suspicions," she said. "Now you're suspicious of *me*."

Evers sighed, shook his head, and began to walk away.

"Where are you going?" she asked.

"I told you, I'm going to have a look around."

"Well, you better take your gun with you. That thing looked pretty vicious."

He nodded, walked to the safe, and pulled out a .38 special caliber revolver. He then walked back to the dining room, turned on the rear lights, opened the sliding glass door and stepped outside. It was a clear night, the smell of blossoming flowers in the air. The only movement was the stirring of the trees in the warm breeze.

Evers walked slowly across the back porch, his eyes wandering from the lighted portion of the yard to the distant trees engulfed in darkness. He was about to turn around when he heard a low growling emanating from the shadows. He held his gun up, and stared toward the trees. Then he listened once again. The warm breeze hissed in his ears.

Lowering the gun, he walked back to the opened door. His wife greeted him as he stepped back inside the house.

"Did you see anything?" she whispered.

"Nothing," he replied.

"Well, I called the police, anyway," she said. "They told me they would send a car over."

"Probably just a waste of time," he muttered, heading back to the safe.

Putting the gun away, he sat down and began reading the newspaper once again. He was about to turn the page when there was a loud crash in the dining room. He heard his wife scream as he jumped up and rushed toward the sound of her voice.

"Carolyn, what the hell happened?" he shouted, racing into the kitchen.

Evers gasped when he saw the shattered glass and his wife in the arms of what looked like a huge tiger, his teeth bared and snarling. He froze for a moment, unable to speak or move, and in that moment, he watched as the tiger growled and then sunk his teeth into his trembling wife's neck . . .

The police car pulled up in front of the Evers' house, the two officers riding inside taking their time, deciding that the call they had received was not any kind of emergency.

"She said it was some kind of prowler," said one of the officers, checking his gun for bullets. "It was probably just a case of nerves."

"I don't doubt it," replied the other officer. "Nothing ever happens in this town."

The other officer laughed, put his hat on, and opened the door. "This won't take long," he said, standing up.

They sauntered down the front walkway, noticing the lights on in the house, and stepped up to the front door. After knocking several times and receiving no answer, they decided they would check around the outside of the house before attempting to get inside. When they finally reached the back of the house, they noticed the shattered glass door. They hurried toward it, removing their guns, and then cautiously stepped across the porch.

One of the officers peered inside the shattered glass. "The house is an absolute wreck," he whispered to his partner. "Definitely an intruder of some kind."

His partner nodded and they carefully bent their bodies through the broken glass, their guns ready to fire. The house was in a state of total disarray, massive scratches along the walls, overturned furniture, and various papers and items scattered throughout. Then they noticed the bodies lying among the debris.

One of the officers stepped up to one of them and gasped. "Why, they've been ripped apart," he said, glancing down at the blood and the mangled flesh.

"What the hell do you suppose it was?" asked his partner with a frown.

"I would say it was the work of some kind of animal," he replied. "Anyway, we'd better call it in."

When the ambulance finally arrived, they carried the bodies out into the faint glow of the moonlight. No one seemed to notice the lone figure moving slowly through the distant trees, his blood-soaked body hidden by the darkness and the shadows. He was heading back from where he had come, hurrying away from the twirling red lights, hoping he would receive help and shelter from those he had come to know. As he approached the old Victorian house, he stumbled, fell to the ground, and finally lay exhausted beneath the glowing moon.

A few yards away, a woman with short, dark hair was running through the darkness. Her movements were frantic, her face filled with fear. She was afraid to shout, to scream, not wanting to disturb the horrible figure she had seen lurking in the woods.

She kept running, not knowing where she was headed, her only thought to find shelter from the unimaginable thing she had seen. She dashed through the trees, and excitedly began knocking on the first door she came to.

"Yes, what can I do for you?" an unusually tall man said, opening the door.

"You have to help me!" screeched the woman. "If it finds me, it will kill me. I don't want to die!"

"Come in, come in," the man said, putting a comforting arm around her. "Now what was it that you saw?"

"Oh, it was horrible," the woman wailed. "It looked like a human being, only it wasn't a human being, it was some sort of animal—"

"There, there," the man said. "It was only your imagination."

"No, no, it was real," the woman insisted. "I watched him as he moved through the woods—"

"An animal, you say?"

"Yes, the largest cat you've ever seen. Something like a tiger. Oh, but it was horrible."

"But you can't really be sure of what you thought you saw," the man replied. "I mean, it was dark and there are shadows in the woods that can produce all kinds of fanciful images."

"No, you must believe me, I know what I saw."

"Okay, but you must relax. When you've had time to think about it for a moment in a calm, rational manner, you might think about it in a different way. Would you like a drink?"

"No, no, I'm fine," the woman answered. She paused for a moment, and sighed. "Those kinds of animals aren't found in this area, are they? No one will really believe me, will they?"

The man smiled. "I'm afraid not," he said. "You just had a fright, it could have been any kind of animal, or even some sort of plant blowing in the wind."

"I guess you're right. How could I have been so foolish?"

"It's all right. People imagine they've seen terrible things all the time. Usually, it turns out to be something very normal."

The woman looked at the man, realized for the first time how tall he was, and turned her head up to glimpse his face.

"Well, you certainly wouldn't be afraid of anything, Mr.—"

"Charlie Endor."

"Well, Mr. Endor, I imagine nothing could scare you. I mean, even if it was a werewolf of some kind you wouldn't be the least frightened."

"No, ma'am."

The woman was beginning to calm down, secure in Endor's presence, when there was a noise at the back door. The woman jumped, and then looked at Endor. "What was that?" she asked.

Endor ignored her question, and slowly walked toward the door. The woman, not wanting to be left alone, sprang from her seat and followed him. Endor opened the door, and from out of the darkness, appeared a panting tiger, standing upright like a man.

"Oh, my God, that's it!" the woman screamed. "That's the monster I saw outside!"

She was about to faint when she quickly turned toward Endor. She looked at him for a moment, jumped back, and her mouth fell open. Somehow Endor had transformed into the tallest bear creature she had ever seen.

The sight of the two monsters was too much for her, and she screamed. Then she swooned, her eyes rolled back, and she fell limply to the floor. Her scream was lost amid the disquieting noises of the night.

"I think we found our man," Detective Dempster was saying, unrolling the newspaper.

Dr. Keld stared at the headline and frowned. COUPLE MANGLED BY MYSTERIOUS INTRUDER. He glanced at the accompanying story and then looked up. "It sounds very much like Kolak," he said. "And not too far from the city. I think we should pay this community a visit, detective, and find out whether Kolak is staying there."

"Exactly what we intended, doctor. I was hoping you would join us. We'll bring the girl and a professor of Eastern Religion that we located. He supposedly knows a lot about shamanism and thinks he can help break Kolak's curse."

"Excellent," said the doctor. "Then I think we should leave as soon as possible. If we're lucky, Kolak sustained some sort of wound during the attack. According to my research, the suspect creature can be exposed by a corresponding injury later apparent on the human. It's known as repercussion, and hopefully, Kolak will have such a marking. If all goes well, we'll locate him and easily prove that he was the one involved in the attack."

"Good, doctor. Then let us prepare to leave."

Dr. Keld nodded and followed the detective out the door and down the hospital corridor. When they reached the front entrance, Dr. Keld could see the black sedan sitting in the road, its windows glistening in the afternoon sun. The detective approached the car, opened the back door, and motioned Dr. Keld to get inside.

"You know Gail," he said. "And this is Dr. Chen. He'll be helping us to break the curse."

Dr. Keld smiled and slid inside. "Very glad to meet you, Dr. Chen," he said. "The detective tells me you're quite versed in the ways of the shaman."

"Yes, that's correct," replied Dr. Chen. "I have studied it all my life. Ever since I was a child in China, shamanism had held a great fascination for me. You see, my people thought of me as a worthy candidate."

"And why is that, Dr. Chen?"

"You see the shaman is supposed to possess special physical and mental characteristics. This includes suffering from some nervous disorder such as epilepsy, or being born with some minor defect—"

"And you have such a defect?"

Dr. Chen nodded. He then held up his hands. The beginnings of a sixth finger protruded from each side of his palms, below the pinkie.

"Extraordinary," said Dr. Keld. "There's no doubt you will be most convincing. It's quite imperative Kolak believe you possess the necessary spiritual powers."

Just then, the motor began to roar, and the car slowly slid down the roadway. "We thought you might be pleased with Dr. Chen," said the detective from behind the steering wheel. "He comes to us with quite impressive credentials."

"I imagine so," replied Dr. Keld. "Then you know something about the disease Kolak suffers from?"

"I know he believes the spirit of the tiger enters his body and controls his soul," said Dr. Chen. "It seems like a simple case of possession."

"Maybe, but I've done a lot of research on the matter and think I should fill you in on what I have found."

"Certainly, doctor."

"You see, those who suffer from lycanthropy believe in a separate soul often appearing in related forms to the original person. This causes them to further believe in such things as the power of witches, vampires, reincarnation of the soul of predatory creatures, such as tigers, alligators, and sharks, and possession by evil spirits."

"It doesn't sound like Roger," interrupted Gail. "I mean, he was very level-headed before he left for Malaysia. You know he was an anthropologist—"

"Yes, yes, my dear, you've told me," replied Dr. Keld. "But something must have happened while he was away in Malaysia, something which affected his brain and changed his value system."

"Many people who you would not suspect are actually very susceptible to the power of suggestion," said Dr. Chen. "The shamans are quite familiar with this particular human failing and use it to their advantage."

"And the one thing they seem to have in common," continued Dr. Keld, "is the desire to defy Nature, to somehow alter it according to their own personal dictates. It's always the same with anyone who believes in the supernatural. They all have a longing for controlling the whims of Nature."

"A most foolish notion," said Dr. Chen. "But human beings have believed in superstition and magic for a very long time."

Dr. Keld nodded. "It's the fervent desire to somehow influence events that are beyond human control. This is especially true during times of personal or social crisis. This was particularly true when life was more precarious and there was a great fear of the unknown. According to my research, lycanthropy was at one time associated with outlawry, and in England and Scandinavia, the term 'berserker' was applied to men who not only suffered from excesses of rage, but who wore garments of bear or wolfskin. In Europe, it was believed that lycanthropy was a deliberate choice to utilize magical means."

"But what would lead Roger to embrace such questionable beliefs?" Gail wondered. "I mean, he was a man of science, a man of learning."

"A man of intellectual curiosity," said Dr. Keld. "It was probably this curiosity which prompted him to explore the ways of lycanthropy, and before he realized it, he had become too deeply involved."

"But a tiger, Dr. Keld? It just seems so fantastic."

"Not really, my dear. According to my research, it was a common belief among the Kols of Central India. In one case, a Kol tried for murder was accused of devouring an entire goat one night and roaring like a tiger. A tiger was then said to have devoured his wife."

"Then we can assume Kolak has become a cannibal of some kind?" asked the detective sitting in the front seat.

"It's quite possible," replied Dr. Keld. "You see, the practice of lycanthropy has been associated with a depraved appetite, including a desire for raw flesh, often that of human beings."

"I refuse to believe it," said Gail. "I mean you're talking about someone I knew quite well for a long time. Roger would never engage in such detestable practices."

"Let's hope so," said Dr. Keld. "Although anything is possible if he did finally succumb to the hallucinations of the *latah*. There are many documented accounts of the eating of human flesh by those suffering from lycanthropy in Africa, as well as Asia."

"Then we must find him as soon as possible and help him," Gail sobbed. "He obviously doesn't know what he's doing. And to think I refused to believe him when he told me he was the victim of some sort of curse. Oh, poor Roger—"

"The real problem is that Roger has already killed," said Dr. Keld with a frown. "And until we find him, I am convinced he will continue to kill."

Gail placed her head in her hands and continued to cry.

"Don't worry, Miss Gail, we will find him," said Dr. Chen, putting his arm around her. "And then I will do everything possible to drive the spirit from his soul."

"But first we must find him," interrupted Dr. Keld. "And to do that, I think we're going to need your help."

Gail stopped crying and looked up. "Yes, doctor," she replied. "I will do anything I can to bring Roger back to his senses."

The doctors smiled as the car rumbled onward beyond the huddled mass of buildings towering above the city.

7

THE OTHER SOUL

KOLAK OPENED HIS EYES AND found he was lying in bed in a strange room, daggers and swords decorating the walls. He sat up and realized there was no longer any blood upon his body, that the proof of his killing spree the night before was totally gone. His blood-soaked clothes had also been taken, replaced by a set of clean pajamas. He swung his legs out of bed and stood on the wooden floor, staring at the drawn black curtains.

Stepping across the floor, he slowly opened the bedroom door, and peered outside into the darkened hallway. He could hear the murmuring of voices downstairs so he slowly made his way to the top of the old wooden staircase and gazed down below. Not able to see anyone, he thought he heard Charlie Endor's voice wafting through the air.

"Charlie?" he finally said, suppressing an urge to shout.

"Charlie?"

After a moment, the tall, burly figure of a man appeared among the shadows.

"Kolak, is that you?"

"Yes, Charlie, it's me. Where am I? Where are my clothes?"

Kolak watched as Endor climbed the stairs, and stood in front of him, looking down, with a benevolent grin across his face. "Relax, Roger," he finally said. "We brought you back inside the house. Your clothes will be ready very soon. We had to wash out the blood."

Kolak sighed. "Then you found me outside this morning?"

"You killed again, Roger," said Endor, becoming serious. "I told you you're going to have to learn how to control your powers if you want to remain alive. You see, it won't be long before the authorities come searching—"

Kolak bowed his head. "I'm sorry, but I have no control over myself once the transformation begins."

"You will learn," replied Endor.

"But how is it possible?"

"You must remain vigilant in subjugating your other soul. It takes practice and discipline."

"But the *latah* is powerful, more powerful than you know."

"You must learn how to control it, Kolak. You must learn before it's too late. I fear that with your latest killing, you don't have much time before they arrive."

"You mean the police?"

"They will come with those you are hiding from, Kolak. Don't you realize they are still searching for you? Now you have given them a clue to your whereabouts. It won't be long before they come looking."

"But they've never come looking for you, Charlie."

"Oh, they did at first. At one time, they chased me halfway around the world. You see, they believed I was the mythical Yeti and that my capture would bring them great fame and fortune. While it's true that when I transform into the bear I leave markings very similar to that monster, I have found many natural bears tend to produce the same imprints. You see, bears sometimes place the hindfoot partly over the imprint of the forefoot, creating what appears to be an enormous human footprint headed in the opposite direction. Anyway, I left behind both human and bear footprints and this eventually caught their attention. But the point is I was finally able to stop running when I discovered I could control my other soul and use it to my advantage. And that, Kolak, is what you must do if you ever wish to live a free and happy life."

Kolak paused for a moment. "Would you be willing to teach me, Charlie?" he finally asked.

"As long as you would be willing to learn quickly, Roger. You see your presence here threatens all of our lives. And if you are unable to control your powers within a reasonable amount of time, I'm afraid everyone in this coven will have to face the consequences."

"Then I'll learn fast. The *latah* has controlled me long enough. I'm tired of prowling through the night and waking up covered in the blood of my victims. And you're right, my latest attack will surely bring the police and those that wish to hunt me down. I'll do everything possible to make sure they fail in their attempts to find me."

"Good, Roger, then I'll give you back your clothes and you'll come downstairs and we'll try to help you."

Kolak nodded and walked back to the room to wait for Endor to return. Several moments later, he received his clothes, hurriedly put them on, and made his way down the old wooden staircase. Several members of the coven met him at the bottom. They were still dressed in their long purple robes.

"Mr. Kolak, it's good to see you again," said one of them, a pretty woman with long brunette hair. Her slender hand was extended in his direction. "My name is Celia Mountainwater. Charlie has told us everything about you and your problem. We're only too willing to assist you."

Kolak expressed his gratitude as each of the members promised their unwavering support. "I hope you remember me, Mr. Kolak," said a woman with large, searing eyes. "I am Lil, Charlie's wife. I, too, am of the turnskin. It was quite difficult for Charlie and I before we learned how to control our other side. But once you embrace the ways of Nature, one is able to understand what is necessary."

"The ways of Nature?" asked Kolak.

"Yes, Mr. Kolak, when one understands the ways of Nature, one possesses the wisdom of the ages. This had been a general principle throughout man's early history, and we of the Wiccan faith, have revived this notion as a central part of our religion. It is quite imperative for you to comprehend this fundamental theory if you are ever to successfully control your other side."

"I will try."

"You must be like water, Mr. Kolak, able to impose your will with the least amount of resistance. That is the only way you will be able to control your other side."

"You said you were able to transform?"

"That is correct, Mr. Kolak. I am like my namesake, Lilith, who was the wind demon of Jewish folklore. She is referred to in the Bible, in Isaiah, as a demon of the desert. In later centuries, she became identified as Adam's first wife. She had been created out of the earth just as Adam had been although she refused to submit to him. When she finally fled and refused to return, God threatened her future children with death, but she still refused vowing she would harm male and female infants. She was what we call a succubus, a fallen angel who later sought mastery over the human race."

"Are you a demon?" asked Kolak.

"I am malignant when I want to be, Mr. Kolak," replied Lil. "You see, I have learned from Nature and from my namesake that one must be like the wind and change directions when necessary. One must also learn when to be silent as a soft breeze and when to howl like the North Wind. It is the wisdom of all natural forces."

"But how do you use these forces to your advantage?"

"It takes time and patience. You must submit yourself to our ways and beliefs. You see, our origins stretch back to the dawn of time when human beings were more curious about their surroundings and worshipped the Goddess. They lived by the ways of Nature and, in time, they became one with it and began to utilize the knowledge they obtained to better their lives and control their surroundings. This is what you must do, Mr. Kolak, to overcome that which possesses your other soul."

"And what about altering Nature?"

"We will do what we can with the use of spells and incantations, but it is you who must resolve to abide by Nature's wisdom."

Kolak nodded, and then glanced at Charlie Endor, who had appeared beside his wife. "Now are you beginning to understand what is necessary in controlling your other soul, Roger?" he asked.

"The ways of Nature," he replied. "I must learn from the wind and the water and all that surrounds me."

"Yes, Roger, and submit yourself to the ways of magic. You must believe you have the power to control your environment and your place in the natural world."

"But do I have enough time?"

"That I cannot say," Endor replied. "But we of the coven will do everything we can to delay the progress of those searching for you and hopefully, give you time to learn."

The others then stepped forward in their long purple robes and pentacles, and one by one, embraced their newest member while chanting the name of the goddess Freya.

One of the women, who was taller than the others and had long brown hair, took hold of Kolak's hand. "This way," she whispered, leading him out the back door.

"Who are you?" Kolak asked, stumbling behind.

"My name is Elizabeth," she replied. "I am also of the turnskin."

"You can change?"

"Yes, it was the greatest thing to ever happen to me. It renewed my soul, and allowed me to enjoy life more than I ever had before."

Kolak grimaced. "But don't you understand that it's a curse?" he said. "Waking up with your body totally drained and the blood of your victim covering the ground beside you—"

"The sex is great," she said with a smile. "There's not a better feeling in all the world when you're a turnskin."

He remembered the last time he made love to a woman, a thin, dark skinned Malaysian woman who treated him like he was a god. There had been others before her. It was all part of the primal ritual of transforming into the beast. The animalistic lust and release, leading to the renewed craving for living flesh. The fertility rites were the culmination of the hunt. Many times they were the prelude to the hunt.

He had promised to stay faithful to Gail, but once in the throes of the ancient ritual, there was little he could do about it. The wild writhing, the banging of the drums, the naked bodies, all combined to cause the barbarous lust to overtake him. Many were wounded in the process, left to die amid the thrashings of sexual desire. The *ecstasy*.

Kolak stared at Elizabeth as she let her purple robe slip from her body. She was totally naked underneath, her ample breasts glistening in the sunlight.

"Take me, Kolak," she said, flinging herself into his arms.

"But you know what can happen," he said. "You know the change can come."

"All the better," she answered. "To feel the beast inside fulfills all our primal sexual desires."

He nodded his head, knowing that was exactly what they believed in Malaysia, the source of the curse. And just like in Malaysia, he couldn't fight the overwhelming desire that was a precursor to the transformation. He wanted to make love, needed it, just as he needed to breathe the warm, fresh air. He had wanted to save himself for Gail, but he wondered if Gail would ever truly understand, and whether he would ever be liberated from the feral beast that hid inside him.

She stepped backwards, and he began unbuttoning his shirt. Just looking at her trim body, her full breasts and small clump of pubic hair, prompted the carnal urge to begin. He undid his pants, and soon he was standing there amid the tall trees and blossoming bushes totally naked, the rigid member straining towards his stomach.

She smiled, got down on all fours, and told him to enter her from behind. That was the way of the mating of the beast.

As he entered her, he could feel the renewed surge of the beast within. She started to pant, and then the transformation began. Her limbs began to change, a soft, brown fur began to sprout across her body. She looked back at him, and he could see the snout appear. She was a werewolf.

He could hear her panting and growling, and then he felt the straining of his muscles, the throbbing of his distended member. He, too, was in the midst of changing, he could feel it swirling inside him.

The rapid growth of hair, the stretching and stressing of his muscles, the enlarging of his teeth, fingers, and nails. He had become the beast once more.

A piercing howl echoed through the woods as Kolak answered with a mighty roar. He was still inside her, bucking wildly, their brutish grunts pulsing through the wind. As the orgasm gripped their bodies, there was a barking of a dog nearby. Kolak turned his head, and could see a boy standing in the distance, holding a leash, a black dog straining forward, his front paws dangling in the air. The boy just stood there, stupefied, watching as the largest tiger he had ever seen copulated with a growling wolf.

"What the—" he could hear the boy exclaim.

Kolak pulled his member from the growling Elizabeth, and then she stood up, very much a snarling wolf, and scampered among the bushes. He could hear the dog now whimpering, and as he turned his head, he could see the boy gasp. He let out another roar, and then the boy turned and ran away, the dog barking as it raced the boy home.

Kolak leaped behind some bushes, and then stared up into the shining sun. He knew the transformation wouldn't last long in the daylight, so he sat down and rested, waiting to change back into a man. In the distance, Elizabeth howled.

"This is where the Evers were killed," the detective said, halting the car and turning back toward the three occupants sitting behind him. "I think we should go inside and take a look around."

"Very good, Detective Dempster," replied Dr. Keld. "We'll certainly be able to determine whether it was Mr. Kolak who perpetrated the crime and possibly where he was headed."

The car doors swung open, and soon, Dr. Keld, Dr. Chen, Gail and the two detectives were standing outside in the midst of a surging breeze. They could see several police cars nearby, and then looked up into the pale gray sky and noticed dark clouds billowing overhead.

"Looks like it's going to rain," said Dr. Keld. "We'd better search the grounds before any of the evidence is washed away."

"Good idea, doctor," answered Dempster. "But we'd better hurry. It doesn't look as if we have much time. I think we should split up and meet again at the back door of the house. I believe that is where the newspaper article said the murderer gained entrance."

They nodded, and then Dr. Keld and Dr. Chen began walking toward the far end of the house, the two detectives and Gail headed in the other direction. After several moments, there was a sudden flash of lightning, and then a burst of thunder, and then the rain came pouring down from the leaden sky.

"We better head to the house," Dr. Chen was shouting as he watched Dr. Keld standing in the slanting rain staring at the ground.

"You go on without me," replied Dr. Keld. "I'll be there in a few more minutes."

Dr. Chen frowned, put his coat over his head, and scrambled through the pelting rain. When he reached the porch, he hurried up the steps and found the back door had already been opened.

"Where's Dr. Keld?" asked Gail, as he stepped inside.

"He's still out there," Dr. Chen replied. "I think he might have found something."

Detective Dempster turned around upon hearing the words. Dr. Chen could see that he and the other detective were standing near two police officers. "He needn't waste his time," the detective finally said. "The officers tell me the grounds have already been checked."

A moment later, Dr. Keld came rushing up the porch steps. Gail handed him a towel as he entered the house. "You're thoroughly soaked, doctor," she said, watching him dry off his glasses and rub the towel against his hair. "I hope it was worth it."

"Most definitely," said Dr. Keld. "I think I found part of a footprint. A cat's print, I might add."

"Good work, doctor," said Dempster. "Could you tell in which direction he was headed?"

"Most certainly, detective," nodded the doctor. "Toward the trees near the front of the house."

"Excellent. Can you officers tell me whether there are houses to the east?"

"A few," one of the officers replied. "But, according to our investigation, it was an animal that murdered these people."

"Quite correct," said the detective. "But what you didn't know was that this animal is actually a man who escaped from the psychiatric hospital."

"A man did all this damage, detective?"

"Not an ordinary man. But a man suffering from a terrible disease that causes him to take the shape of a tiger."

"Are you quite serious?" asked one of the officers. "I've never heard of such a disease."

"It's actually quite rare," interrupted Dr. Keld. "But it does exist, officer. It's known as pathological lycanthropy. And after looking over some of the damage left behind, I would certainly have to say that it was Mr. Kolak who caused it."

"You mean, including those scratches along the wall?"

"Yes, most definitely," replied Dr. Keld. "As I said, Mr. Kolak's terrible disease causes him to take the shape of an animal resembling a tiger. While in this state, he's capable of enormous destruction, like what you see here, much like what a normal tiger would be capable of."

"Well, it's still pretty hard to believe," said one of the officers. "But if you're right, I think we should begin checking some of those houses."

"Exactly what I had in mind," said Dempster. "If this is the work of Kolak, we should be able to find him hiding in one of them."

"Take two officers with you, detective. That way, your search will go that much faster. If you need any additional assistance, don't hesitate to ask us."

The detective nodded and then led the small group toward the door. The rain had changed to a light drizzle as they headed for the cars.

"He might be staying with someone he knows," said Dr. Keld, as they hurried down the driveway. "We must consider such a possibility since we know someone must have driven him away from the city to this area."

"You may be right, doctor," replied Dempster. "We'll make sure to keep things calm to quiet their suspicions."

"The only problem is if Kolak sees us, he'll know immediately why we've come."

"Let us handle this, doctor. First, we have to find Kolak, and then we'll decide the best way to capture him."

"You're not going to shoot him, are you?" asked Gail.

"We'll do everything possible to bring him back alive," replied the detective. "But you must understand, my dear, that Roger has already murdered several people and we must do anything we can to end the killing once and for all."

"Don't worry, Miss Gail," said Dr. Chen. "It is very difficult to kill one possessed by the animal spirit."

"Yes, I believe you need silver bullets or fire to burn out the demonic soul," said Dr. Keld.

"How horrible," gasped Gail. "Isn't there any other way?"

"That, my dear, is exactly why Dr. Chen has come along. If we can only convince Roger to give up peacefully, we can try to drive the demonic spirit from his soul."

"If he believes the shaman can help him, doctor," said Dempster. "Only if he believes in superstition and magic as much as you think he does."

"That's why I must speak with him, detective. I must explain to him that the shaman is his only chance to be rid of the spirit."

"And if he refuses?"

"Then I'll leave it to you to do what you must, detective."

"I will explain it to him," interrupted Gail. "He will listen to me. He *must* listen to me."

"That is, if we're the first ones to find him," said the detective. "You see, these officers are going to be helping us with our search."

"Don't worry, miss, we'll do what we can to bring him back alive," said one of the officers.

Gail smiled, realizing these men were ready to help Roger. "If I can only get him to listen to reason," she said. "Then maybe he would give himself up and we could possibly end this curse of his."

"We're prepared to do everything we can to make Roger realize that there is still hope," replied Dr. Keld.

When they reached the car, Dr. Chen, Gail and Dr. Keld opened the back doors and slid inside. The two detectives sat down in the front seat and then Detective Dempster made the motor snarl. They could see the two officers getting into their car as they started down the driveway.

"Now this may be dangerous, folks," said the younger detective, staring out the window as the trees slid by. "So I think all three of you should stay in the car when we begin our search."

"But we must surely follow you, Detective Coggs," said Dr. Keld. "I think Roger would listen to us. Besides, the sight of police detectives might actually cause him to do something irrational. Our presence may help to prevent unnecessary violence."

"The doctor may be right," replied Dempster. "If he sees them with us, he might decide to talk. But I must caution you to stay behind us at all times in case there's any sort of violence."

"You have our word, detective," said Dr. Keld.

As they continued on their way, it began to rain once again, harder and harder, until they were in the midst of a steady downpour. The raindrops pattered against the car windows, silence overtaking the occupants inside, as the constant thump of the windshield wipers echoed among them. They squinted through the falling rain, trying to spot a dwelling of some kind, when Detective Coggs suddenly began to shout.

"There! Behind those trees!" he said.

Sure enough, they all turned to glimpse a white house peeking out from among a clump of trees. Dempster slowly pulled down the long driveway, and then when he finally reached the structure, he stopped the motor and reached for his gun.

"I'll only use it if I have no other choice," he said, turning toward the back seat. "It's going to be up to you three to get him out of there alive."

"Don't worry, detective," said Gail. "Roger will talk to me. I know he'll talk to me."

"Okay, then, let's get going," he replied.

They opened the doors, and soon, the two doctors and Gail were following the detectives up the walkway. When they reached the front door, they halted as one, took a deep breath, and Detective Dempster began to knock.

Several moments passed and then the door slowly opened. A man with dark stubble stood there in the doorway in a white undershirt looking at them with a pair of dark, scornful eyes.

"What d'ya want?" he grumbled.

"We're from the New York City police department," said the detective, holding up his badge in the falling rain. "We're looking for a Roger Kolak. Do you happen to know him?"

"I don't know nobody," sneered the man.

"I must tell you Mr. Kolak is a wanted fugitive. It would be better for all of us if you just decided to cooperate."

"You got the wrong guy," he replied with a grimace. "Just like you pigs to screw up." The man then backed up and began closing the door.

"If you see him, tell him we want to speak to him. Got it?"

Before the detective could utter another word, the door suddenly snapped shut.

"I don't think he's in there," said Gail. "I can just feel it."

"Hopefully not," said Dempster, turning and walking back to the car.

The small group followed him until they were once again inside rolling down the street.

"And why didn't you think he was in there, Gail?" asked the detective, the thump of the windshield wipers rising above his voice.

"He just seemed a little too sleazy for Roger to associate with," she replied. "I don't think he would ever consider getting involved with such a coarse man."

"You must realize Roger has changed, my dear," said Dr. Keld. "Who knows what kind of person he would be associated with at this particular time?"

Gail winced. "I would hate to think Roger has sunk that low, doctor," she finally said.

The conversation might have continued if not for a sudden streak of lightning and a blast of thunder. The occupants fell silent once more as the car rolled onward. Then, without warning, the detective slowly pulled up to the side of the road, glancing to his right.

"I think I saw a house when that lightning lit up the sky," he said. "Right over there, behind those trees."

They looked toward where he was pointing, and then another bolt of lightning sizzled through the air.

"Yes, we saw it," said Gail from behind. "It's dark brown. You can hardly see it with all this rain and the trees in front."

"Well, we'd better check it out," said the detective. "Looks like it's close enough to the Evers' house."

Another bolt of lightning flashed before them, accompanied by the roar of thunder, as the car crept up the driveway. They could soon see the dark brown Victorian house standing behind a clump of swaying tree limbs. Dempster finally stopped the car, and the small group opened the doors and huddled together beneath the ominous sky. The detectives than led the way toward the front door and, amid the falling raindrops and the crack of thunder, they began to knock.

After several moments, the door slowly opened revealing a female with black hair wearing a long purple robe.

"How may I assist you?" she inquired.

"We are looking for a man you may know," said the detective. "His name is Roger Kolak—"

The female frowned. "I am sorry but there is no one here who answers to that name," she finally responded. "Perhaps, if you tell me what he looks like—"

Before the detective could reply, Dr. Keld grabbed Gail by the arm and hurriedly stepped forward.

"You see, we are friends of Roger's," explained the doctor. "Gail here was supposed to marry him—"

"But as I told you, there is no one by that name here in this house."

"We know," said Dr. Keld. "But, you see, we heard Roger was in the area and Gail here was worried something might have happened to him. She only wishes to talk to him, tell him that she still loves him, and will do anything to convince him to return to her."

"But, as I said, Mr. Kolak is not among us—"

"But if you do see him, you will tell him Gail is looking for him, will you not?"

"Of course," she nodded.

She then grabbed the door and closed it, as another bolt of lightning crackled in the sky.

"What was that all about, doctor?" asked Dempster, as they headed back to the car.

"I believe he's in that house," the doctor replied. "I'm almost certain, detective."

As they got back inside the car, the detective continued his inquiry. "But how could you know, doctor?" he asked.

The doctor leaned forward with an anxious pause. "Did you see what the girl was wearing around her neck?" he finally said.

"It looked like a small necklace of some kind," the detective replied.

"Not just any necklace," said the doctor. "But a pentacle, the five-pointed star of the witch and the turnskin."

"Yes, I saw it," gushed Gail. "Then you think they're hiding Roger inside that house?"

"I think it's quite certain," the doctor replied. "You see, the pentagram is a symbol of magic, used by those who wish to alter Nature, or themselves, I might add."

"Dr. Keld is quite correct," said Dr. Chen. "The pentagram has been used for possession for a very long time."

"Then I think we better stay close," said Dempster, backing the car down the driveway. "The only problem is not being detected in doing so."

"But somehow I think Kolak will want to find us now," said Dr. Keld. "Somehow I believe he's still in love with Gail."

They looked at him, the raindrops continuing to fall through the misty air, and then before another word could be spoken, a great clap of thunder rumbled in the distant sky.

8

THE DECISION

"THEY HAVE COME FOR YOU, Mr. Kolak," said the female with black hair. "They said there is someone named Gail looking for you."

"Gail? She was with them?" Kolak bowed his head.

"There was a female with them," she replied. "I believe it was the one known as Gail."

"Then I have to go out and see her. I'll talk to her before anything happens that I might regret."

He could see Lil watching him, and then suddenly step forward. "You are in love with this one?" she asked.

"At one time," Kolak replied. "Although now, after all that's happened . . . I just don't know anymore."

"If you love her, you must take her," said Lil. "She would make a fine receptacle for your child, Mr. Kolak. The legendary Merlin was said to have been the offspring of such a union."

"But you don't understand. Gail was going to be my wife. I was in love with her—"

"Excellent," cooed Lil. "She will be the perfect mother for your offspring."

"And what about the others?'

"We will take care of them, Mr. Kolak. They are only ordinary human beings."

"But I'm not ready yet. I still haven't learned to control my other soul."

"We will take care of it, Mr. Kolak."

He looked at Charlie Endor, who glared back at him. "What's the problem, Roger?" he asked. "Do you have misgivings about destroying these people who are your avowed enemies?"

Kolak instinctively shook his head. "I have no concern for the others, Charlie, they can go to Hades, but Gail is with them . . . don't you understand? I was in love with her at one time . . . I can't bring myself to approve of her destruction."

"Then you must go and see her," Endor replied. "You must go and talk to her if you must."

"But the others, they seek to destroy me. And even if they don't kill me, they wish to take me back to that hospital."

"Then we must destroy them before they destroy you," Endor said. "You are much more valuable to us, Roger, than you know—"

"But what about Gail? I need to explain it to her, make her understand what has happened. I owe her that much."

"Is it quite necessary, Mr. Kolak?" interjected Lil. "Is she really worth your undying concern? Has this woman understood anything up until this point?"

Kolak grimaced.

"I thought not," continued Lil. "You say she loves you, and yet, she has done everything possible to aid your enemies. And now they have found you, Mr. Kolak, and she has done nothing to try to stop them from destroying you. Is that love, Mr. Kolak?"

"She never fully understood what had happened to me," replied Kolak. "But throughout it all, she continued to profess her love."

"Then I think you have a problem, Roger," said Endor. "Because, you see, you're going to have to decide what to do about the situation, and whether you love Gail enough to protect her from certain danger. And you must decide all this in a very short amount of time."

Kolak looked at him, searching for a reply, and then glanced gloomily toward the window.

"We cannot die, Kolak."

He looked at Elizabeth, her long brown hair shimmering in the light. "As much as they try, they cannot kill us."

"And what happens to our other soul?"

Elizabeth laughed, a hissing savage laugh. "It grows along with us, Kolak," she said. "Guided by the full moon, and the smell of blood in the air."

"And you don't see that as a curse?" he asked.

Elizabeth smiled. "It's more of a blessing than you know, Kolak," she said. "When I change, my senses are more acute and my will to survive is more unyielding. There is nothing on this earth that can disturb my utter contentment of being alive. Surely, you have felt it, too, Kolak."

"But there is this need inside to be normal again. There were so many plans I made—"

"With that woman?" Elizabeth sneered.

"Gail and I were planning to be happy together," he replied. "We were going to live a normal, happy life."

Elizabeth grimaced. "You don't need an ordinary being any longer, Kolak," she said. "She'll only get in your way, prevent you from doing what it is you were meant to do."

"No, Gail gave me her love and support—"

"She can't give you what you really need, Kolak. Take me, I am the one who can help you, strengthen you—"

"Then it will never end—"

"It's not supposed to end, Kolak. It's supposed to be developed, refined, controlled, until it becomes an integral part of your soul."

"No, it will overtake me. The beast is too strong, too willful. It knows only the smell of blood and the taste of human flesh."

"Yes, it knows who are the true beasts among man and woman."

Kolak bowed his head. "I want only to know the love of a good woman," he said. "Gail could provide that for me."

"She'll never understand your affliction, Kolak," Elizabeth sneered. "She'll only seek to limit you, make you what she wants."

"And you, Elizabeth? Could you really provide the love necessary for a trusting relationship?"

"I may be a werewolf, Kolak, but I am not devoid of love. Besides, among our kind, it is more the sex that keeps us together. Did you not enjoy the love we shared, Kolak?"

"It's a shallow love, wild and untamed."

"It can lead to deeper emotion, Kolak."

"But it can never be the same as normal love. There's too much savagery, a selfish will to survive, involved."

Elizabeth frowned, snarled as the wolf she would become, and angrily walked away.

"How long shall we wait, detective?" asked Dr. Keld, watching the raindrops spatter against the window and then create tiny rivulets that shimmied toward the ground.

"Well, we must first make sure that he's in there before we take any action," he replied. "Once we spot him, we'll have a reason to go inside."

"Somehow I don't think they'll make it easy for us," said the doctor. "You see, I believe those living inside that house are practicing witchcraft."

"And what leads you to that belief, doctor?"

"The robe and the pentacle that woman was wearing are items associated with such practices, detective. You see, in researching lycanthropy, I was led to many passages explaining magic, superstition, and, yes, witchcraft. The actual word, 'witch,' refers to the art or craft of the wise, it being a form of 'wit,' to know."

"Then you think their intentions are evil, doctor?"

"According to my research, detective, modern witchcraft is entirely different from the satanic groups imagined by those who opposed it in past centuries. Today it is called, 'wicca,' supposedly an early Anglo-Saxon word for witchcraft, and it is said to embrace such themes as the love of nature, the equality of male and female, and a belief in magic."

"That's what they claim, doctor, but anyone engaging in magic is naturally prone to evil ends."

"That's exactly what the early Church believed, detective. They called it a delusion and a deception and that it opposed the notion that only God was powerful enough to control Nature. You see, they believed that if one doubted the power of God, then they were aligning themselves with Satan as an equal opponent. It was then witchcraft began to be associated with demonic possession, heresy, and the rejection of God, and became the focus of the Inquisition in the thirteenth century. It was then the image of these supposed representatives of evil began to emerge."

"They were treated horribly, weren't they, doctor?" asked Gail.

"Well, according to the theologians of the late Middle Ages, it was impossible for natural miracles to take place and therefore, anything supernatural and not of God must be the product of collusion with Satan or his minions. And thus began the 'witch craze' that swept through Europe from about 1450 to 1700, resulting in the deaths of thousands of people, mostly innocent women, who were supposedly proven to practice sorcery in allegiance to Satan or who confessed after cruel tortures. The public trials and executions were usually based on the biblical phrase from Exodus that 'you shall not permit a witch to live,' and edicts issued by the Pope. It all culminated in colonial America in 1692 when the Salem witch trials took place as a result of accusations by a group of teen-age girls. Twenty people were executed as a result of the trials, many after torture."

"Well, we don't plan on executing or torturing them, doctor," said the detective. "But we will arrest them if they're found to have been harboring a wanted fugitive such as Kolak."

"I understand, detective," replied the doctor. "I just wanted all of you to know something about the people we may be dealing with. If these are witches, then they probably know something about the past, and may use any part of that knowledge against us in attempting to prevent their capture."

Dempster frowned, turning toward the doctor. "You don't really believe in all that hocus-pocus—"

"I must confess I was quite skeptical until I personally witnessed Mr. Kolak's transformation at the hospital. Now I think it's prudent to believe anything is possible."

The detective snorted in disdain.

"Anyway, it's for Dr. Chen to decide whether it's true or not," the doctor continued. "For he's the one who must perform the possession ceremony."

They turned toward Dr. Chen and noticed his tranquil demeanor. "I will do what I must," he calmly said.

"Have you come to a decision, Mr. Kolak?"

Kolak quickly turned around, and stared into Lil's piercing gaze.

"I don't know," he finally murmured. "I just don't want any of you to get hurt as a result of anything I might decide to do."

"Do not worry yourself over us, Mr. Kolak. We are quite able to take care of ourselves in the event of any sort of mishap. It is you who must decide whether this woman is worth your concern."

"I think I still love her—"

"Then you must do what your heart tells you to do. In the meantime, we have taken steps to make certain the others will not harm you."

He glanced at Lil's hands and noticed she was holding some sort of figure made of wax in one and a silver knife in the other.

"These were first used in Egypt," she said, holding up the wax figure. "There was a trial of women and officers of the harem of Rameses III and they were found to have made wax images of the Pharaoh. A very useful charm to gradually destroy one's enemies."

"This, on the other hand, Mr. Kolak," she said, referring to the knife, "is one of the only weapons that can actually kill beings like us. It is made from the silver of a melted crucifix."

He watched as she sauntered toward one of the candles and held the figure over the flame. After a few moments, part of it began to melt.

"Who is it supposed to be?" asked Kolak.

"This, Mr. Kolak, is the image of that detective who was inquiring about you. I think it is a most acceptable likeness, don't you agree? I imagine that poor man's soul will be destroyed before too long, and you, Mr. Kolak, will be free of him."

He stared at the figure and noticed it was quite similar to the detective he had seen at the hospital.

"You see, there are many ways one may bring harm to one's enemies without the use of physical violence," she said. "The texts to conjure up demons are contained in very old handbooks that come to us from centuries past. Even before the burning times. They are known as the grimoires, and were first used to help the magician outwit the demons in order to avoid submitting to their end of the bargain. They were supposed to have been used by the legendary King Solomon, and the greatest of all grimoires is, indeed, known as 'The Key of Solomon.' This and grimoires from Egypt have been passed down to us through the ages."

"There's another book, isn't there?"

"The Book of Shadows," replied Lil. "It's the book of our beliefs, witchcraft laws, rituals, herbal and healing laws, incarnations, chants, dances, divination methods, spells, and Sabbath rites. This book, Mr. Kolak, must be kept secret at all times, and is kept by the High Priestess or High Priest."

"Then there must be something in there about removing a curse," said Kolak.

"There is, my friend, but we had hoped you would come to accept this curse and use it for the good of the coven."

"Then am I damned to live like this my entire life?"

"You will get used to it, Mr. Kolak. It is the source of your power."

Kolak looked at her, and then the conversation was suddenly interrupted by one of the other females.

"Those that wish to destroy you, Mr. Kolak, are sitting inside their car, which is parked across the street."

Kolak slowly walked to the window. "And Gail is with them," he finally said.

"Yes, the female is inside."

He stared through the window, the windswept rain spilling across the glass, and attempted to catch a glimpse of Gail's face.

"There are four others," he said.

"And they will wait, Mr. Kolak. They will wait until they find you."

He kept looking through the window, until finally he turned, and slowly walked away.

"There's a man at the window," said Detective Dempster, staring into the binoculars. "I think it might be him."

"It probably is," said Dr. Keld. "But I suppose we must be sure before we do anything about it."

Gail leaned forward upon hearing the words. "Let me see, detective," she said. "I'll tell you whether it's Roger or not."

The detective nodded, handing her the glasses. She pointed them at the window, and through the falling drops of rain, attempted to observe the figure. She soon realized there was no longer anyone there.

"He's gone," she said, scanning the rain-soaked window. "He knows we're waiting for him."

"Then I think we should prepare ourselves for a possible confrontation," said Dr. Keld. "It won't be long before we find out whether he wants to be located."

He looked at the detective, and saw he had slumped forward against the steering wheel. Detective Coggs was reaching over, attempting to assist him.

"Detective, are you all right?" asked the doctor.

The detective groaned, placing his hand on the back of his neck. "I don't know what it is," he murmured. "I seem to be burning up."

Coggs leaned over and began rolling down the window. "This should revive you," he said.

"Never mind about me," replied Dempster. "Keep watching that house."

Coggs nodded, and glanced through the open window, when there was a sudden tapping on the rear window next to Dr. Chen. They turned around as one, except for Dempster, and could see a man standing there glaring at them. Gail gasped at the sight of him and then began to shout.

"Roger!" she said.

9

THE POWER OF THE SHAMAN

THEY WALKED HAND IN HAND, across the glistening street, the rain still falling all around them like a heavy sigh. The others waited behind, knowing only she could convince him to submit to their demands. They walked past the dim puddles, the raindrops splashing amid the gleaming reflections and rippling outward in silent echoes, and then he halted, pulled her hand toward him and groaned.

"Oh, Gail, I tried to explain it to you," he said, his emotions in disarray. "But it was too horrible, too incredible. I didn't want to scare you, hurt you, anymore than I had to. I figured you would eventually learn the truth, anyway. But I had to know whether you still loved me."

"But I still do," she insisted, letting her hand slowly glance against his lips. "And I still want to help you, Roger. I told you I would do anything for you as long as I could help you—"

"Is that why you brought those men to me? To help me?"

"Yes, Roger, they want to help," she moaned, a tear spilling from her eye and merging with the falling rain. "They know all about the disease you suffer from and swear they can cure you. Oh, you must listen, before harm comes to anyone else."

"But they want to put me back in the hospital, Gail. I can't let them do that. I won't let them do that to me again."

"But they're going to help you, Roger—"

"With medications and talk of suicide?" He looked at her, grabbed her by the arms, and stared into her deep blue eyes. "Don't you understand? It's not a disease that you can simply cure by taking some pill. It's a curse, Gail, something I must learn to live with."

"But Dr. Chen can help you," she sobbed. "He's willing to try to remove the curse—"

"Dr. Chen? Who is he, another psychiatrist?"

"He knows about the shaman, Roger," she said, her voice brimming with concern. "He said his people consider him a shaman and that he knows how to remove the curse."

Kolak let go of her arms and turned away. "A shaman," he murmured. "But that's impossible. What's he doing here, now?"

She stepped toward him, placing her hand upon his shoulder. "Oh, Roger, I wouldn't lie to you," she said. "The detectives found him, they said he is an expert in Eastern Religion. He knows all about the shaman and that terrible curse he placed on you. He wants to help you, Roger. Don't you see? It may be your last chance to become yourself again. You don't have to live the rest of your life tormenting your soul. There's still hope—"

"Hope, Gail? By placing my soul in some lecturer's hands who knows nothing but theories he picked up in some archaic textbook? He probably has never even seen a shaman before—"

"That's not the Roger I once knew," she replied, turning away. "The Roger I knew was fascinated with all the possibilities life had to offer. He was interested in the great forum of ideas, never willing to discard one without considering another. He was intrigued by man's astonishing development through the ages, always seeking to discover the secret of his undying faith. That Roger would have been more than willing to explore the possibilities of a new theory, even if it had been concocted in the closed doors of the laboratory. That Roger knew that every theory carries with it a kernel of truth that must be examined and verified in the grand laboratory of life. Yes, that Roger would have listened and considered every possible option presented to him."

When she had finished speaking, Kolak turned, put his arm around her, and kissed her with a fervor he had long forgotten. "That Roger would have been very much in love with you, Gail," he finally whispered. "He knew you shared much of his passion for exploring the unknowns of human existence. That Roger would have believed anything you had to say, knowing in his heart that you only had his best interests in mind. Yes, that Roger would have listened, my darling. He would have followed you to the ends of the earth if that was your desire."

"Then listen to me now, Roger," she pleaded. "It isn't too late. There's still time to reclaim your soul. You mustn't reject this opportunity. It may be your last, my darling. Oh, I beg you!"

The rain continued to fall, sprinkling their faces and hair, and tapping against the ground in a gentle rhythm. He grabbed her hand and led her to a large, spreading tree, and they stood there beneath the swaying limbs staring into each other's eyes.

"I don't know if the others would allow it," he finally said, casting his eyes toward the speckled soil.

"Dr. Keld says they are practicing witchcraft—"

"They believe in the ways of Nature, Gail. They're helping me to control my other soul."

She frowned. "Then you are resigned to living with this curse for the rest of your life?" she asked.

"I don't know," he said with a shake of his head. "I just don't know. They tell me there are great powers involved, powers I can eventually control and use to my advantage—"

"Oh, don't you see what will happen, Roger?" she said. "This disease, this curse, will eventually overwhelm you and hold your soul prisoner forever. Is that the power you desire? These people, they, too, are prisoners. They're being held captive by superstition and magic and the delusion that they somehow can control the world around them."

"But I've seen their magic—"

"It's all deception and coincidence, Roger. I thought you would know better. I once respected your scientific mind, but now I see you have given it all up for the promise of unbridled power. Can this be so?"

He looked at her with renewed admiration, knowing her words were filled with truth and unmitigated concern for his welfare. "Well, he would have to perform the ceremony inside that house," he finally said. "It's my only chance."

"But can the others be trusted? Will they allow such a ceremony to take place?"

"I'll have to explain it to them. They'll understand, I know they will. But don't you see? If I go with you before any kind of ceremony, they'll undoubtedly throw me back inside that hospital. I can't take the chance that they're only using that supposed shaman as bait."

She sighed and then attempted to smile. "Then we'll have the ceremony inside that house, Roger," she said. "If it pleases you, I'll be there to watch you redeem your soul."

A jubilant grin spread across his face as he stepped forward and held her in his arms. "Nothing would please me more," he said. She then held his hand and led him back to the waiting vehicle as the raindrops fluttered all around them.

When they reached the car, they opened the back door and only Gail slid inside. "And what about you, Mr. Kolak, are you coming with us?" asked Dr. Keld.

"We've decided to hold the ceremony inside that house," replied Kolak, pointing across the street. "All of Dr. Chen's needs will be taken care of. I only hope he is who he says he is."

"You're in no position to make any kind of demands or threats, Kolak," said Detective Dempster, holding a handkerchief to his forehead. "We should throw you in the car and take you back to the city right now."

Kolak smiled. "But you won't do that, will you, detective?" he said. "You won't do that because you know the people in that house wouldn't take kindly to such an action—"

"You think I'm afraid of those so-called witches, Kolak?" shouted the detective. "They're all just psychos as far as I'm concerned with no greater powers than any of us."

"But are you willing to take that chance? I see you're not feeling so well, detective. What on earth is the problem?"

The detective sneered. "Just a temporary thing, Kolak. It's nothing for you to worry about. I'm quite well enough to haul your ass back to prison at any time—"

"Please, detective, you're not helping the situation," said Gail from the back seat. "Roger is quite willing to partake in the ceremony now. That's what we all hoped for. It's best if we allow Dr. Chen to make the necessary preparations. Then we can all go back to the city in peace."

"You wouldn't be afraid, detective, that I may transform into the beast while we were headed back?" Kolak asked with a grin.

"Now, now, Mr. Kolak," interrupted Dr. Keld. "Our only objective is to rid you of that terrible curse and help you readjust to the life you once knew."

Kolak looked at him and grinned. "Very good, doctor," he said.

"If you truly want to break your curse, Mr. Kolak, then we must make a serious and single-minded effort."

Kolak glared at the other man in the back seat who had made the statement and grimaced. "And this, no doubt, is the eminent Dr. Chen," he said. "I hope, for your sake, you truly can command the powers of the shaman, doctor."

"I was chosen by the spirits a long time ago, Mr. Kolak. You see, I encountered Erlen Khan himself at a very early age."

"Erlen Khan, doctor?"

"He who commands the wicked gods of the Underworld, Mr. Kolak. He confronted me in a vision while I was still young and proceeded to torment me for months. It is then I fell into the 'long sleep,' whereupon he cut me into pieces and counted my bones."

"And what did he find, doctor?" asked Kolak.

"That I had an extra bone and was, indeed, worthy of being a shaman. You see, Mr. Kolak, I also have six fingers on each hand." Dr. Chen held up his hands, allowing Kolak to examine them.

"Very impressive, doctor, you may actually be who you say you are," he finally replied.

The shaman. He had first seen him in the Malaysian forest standing there and grinning at him, his teeth glinting in the pale sunlight. He had more teeth than he had ever seen in one mouth before. "It is the sign of the shaman," one of the Malays had said. He stood there in his ritual gown, consisting of the skin of tigers, holding a drum, metal rattlers, and a long wooden staff. "I have been expecting you, Kolak," he had said. Then he had explained to him that the spirits had informed him of his arrival and that they had insisted he teach this "white man from the other side" all about them. "You have been chosen to carry the tiger spirit," he had said . . .

"I must be undisturbed when I perform the ceremony," Dr. Chen was now saying, standing there in the misty rain. "The *lupa* is very strong. One must not be disturbed when appealing to the spirits."

Kolak stared into his eyes, could detect the ways of the shaman glistening inside. "And what spirits will you be appealing to, doctor?" he asked.

"I will be appealing to Ulgen, god of the Upper World, and Erlen Khan, Mr. Kolak," replied Dr. Chen. "But I fear the eastern gods will be more helpful in freeing you from the *latah*."

Kolak paused for a moment to consider the doctor's words. "And when do we get started?" he finally asked.

Dr. Chen stared at him, a solemn expression he associated with the Yonder World etched upon his face. "We already have, Mr. Kolak," he replied.

The candles flickered at the four cardinal points, north, south, east and west, as the members of the coven formed a circle and appealed to the spirits beyond. Kolak watched them as they chanted the names of the gods, and then stepped forward through the symbolic gate. He glanced at Charlie Endor and Lil and wondered whether they had approved the shaman ceremony. After a few moments, they stood up, extinguished the candles, and ritually closed the circle.

"Well, what have you decided?" asked Kolak, as he walked beside Endor and his wife.

"You're quite sure this shaman of yours can invoke the spirits, Roger?" replied Endor.

"Well, he seems to possess some of the necessary peculiarities. I mean, he supposedly has extra bones in his body and I saw the six fingers on each of his hands. He said he was chosen by the spirits at an early age."

"So he has encountered the spirits before," murmured Endor. "And you say he can command the tiger spirit possessing your soul?"

"That's what he claims—"

"And you're quite sure you want to rid yourself of this spirit?" interjected Lil. "I mean, we've explained to you how important it is to the coven and how you could learn to use it—"

"Don't try to talk him out of it, Lil," said Endor. "If Roger thinks he will live a better life without his other soul, then that's his decision. I just hope Gail is as special as he thinks she is."

"But she is," insisted Kolak. "I love her very much and she still seems to care about me."

"Did you explain to her the nature of your powers?" asked Lil. "Does she realize the great potential involved?"

Kolak looked down. "She seems to think these powers will eventually overwhelm me and imprison my soul—"

"But doesn't she know we're here to help you?" interrupted Lil. "That we'll be guiding you until you learn how to take control of this enormous power?"

"No, you don't understand," Kolak said with a shake of his head. "Gail is reluctant to place her trust in magic. She doesn't think it wise to attempt to control the ways of Nature."

They fell silent for a moment, and then Lil looked at him with a malevolent gleam in her dark, penetrating eyes. "She does not believe in our abilities?" she finally asked.

"I think she doesn't trust them," he replied.

Lil frowned. "Then she has never seen you as the tiger, Mr. Kolak?"

"She only knows what the doctors told her."

"I see," she said. "Then she also doubts your powers."

"I don't really know," he replied.

"Well, then, I think it's only right for you to allow her to witness the possession ceremony. She'll then begin to understand the extent of the powers involved."

"Yes, yes, I quite agree," said Endor. "We'd all like to meet Gail, anyway."

"And the shaman?" asked Kolak.

"Tell him he can begin at any time," replied Endor. "We won't do anything to prevent the ceremony from taking place."

Kolak nodded and headed for the door. As he opened it, he motioned toward the car, and moments later Dr. Chen stepped out of the shadows. He was wearing a long, white gown partially hidden by a white apron and carrying a drum. In one of his hands was a wooden drumstick decorated with various human and animal figures. Huddled behind him were Gail and Dr. Keld, the detectives standing behind them with their lips curled in derisive sneers.

"Okay, Kolak, let's get this show on the road," said Dempster with a jeering smirk. "We don't want to keep the spirits waiting."

Kolak noticed the rain had ceased, a misty twilight now sweeping down from the dark, grim clouds above. He then glanced at Gail, who returned his gaze somewhat apprehensively.

"Isn't this what you wanted?" he asked her.

"I just pray the ceremony is a success," replied Gail. "If you only knew how much I want to see you free of this dreadful curse—"

Her voice trailed off into a low moan as the shaman held the drumstick in the air and stepped inside the house. "The spirits are quite active," he announced, as if taking the spiritual pulse of the building.

"That's because we utilize the spirits ourselves," explained Lil, edging toward him. "It is called the evocation."

The shaman continued moving forward, surveying all that surrounded him. He glanced at the pentagram etched upon the floor and the daggers hanging upon the wall and, without a word, shuffled through the house. He finally halted in front of Charlie Endor, and peered toward the top of his head. Endor looked down with an affable gleam in his eyes.

"You are the shaman," he said. "I had a vision of your impending arrival. A monition of your approach."

"The aura is strong here," replied Dr. Chen. "The spirits will be most content."

"And who are these spirits?" asked Endor.

"They are of two worlds, east and west, but I believe those of the east and of Erlen Khan will be most useful in cleansing these grounds."

"That's not what you were sent for, shaman. You're here only to take possession of Mr. Kolak's tiger soul."

"Precisely," murmured Dr. Chen.

"Then you are aware of the other soul, shaman?"

"But there are several souls," corrected the doctor. "There is a soul one reveals when staring into water, and another when the sun is shining, as well as those of good and evil."

"And you're prepared to rescue the one of the tiger spirit?"

"That is my intention."

Kolak watched as Endor moved toward Gail, who was standing near the doorway. He quickly made his way across the room, hoping to hear what Endor would say to her. He could see Gail looking up at the towering figure and smiling.

"Well, I'm most glad to meet you, my dear," said Endor. "Roger has told us so much about you. My name's Charlie Endor, I was the one who found Roger by the side of the highway."

"I'm most pleased to meet you, Mr. Endor," she said, holding out her hand. "I'm sure Roger is very grateful for your assistance."

"Call me Charlie. I've come to know Roger quite well. I understand you're not pleased with his powers."

Gail frowned. "His powers, Charlie, have already caused many deaths and untold damage," she said. "It's a curse that must be broken if Roger is to live again."

"It is my opinion Roger started living when he discovered the powers he now possesses."

"That's only your opinion, Charlie," replied Gail, attempting to hide her anger and her fear.

"Yes, but we've come to respect Charlie's opinion about many things," said a female voice from behind.

Gail turned around and stared into Lil's penetrating gaze. "And you also believe Roger would be better off being a captive of a shaman's curse?"

Lil smiled. "What I believe, miss, is that you have convinced Roger that his powers are not of any measurable value."

"But they're not. They've only caused death and sorrow and have ruined both of our lives."

"That's because Roger has never learned how to properly control them," replied Lil. "You see, my husband and I, my name being Lil, were prepared to guide Roger in utilizing those powers to his advantage."

"Well, Lil, I don't think those powers, as you call them, can ever be used for the good of anyone, except one intending evil."

Lil stared into her eyes, grimaced, and turned away. Kolak watched as she walked toward Charlie Endor, a malicious grin appearing on her face. He then glanced at Gail. What was she thinking? Probably wondering how he could actually *like* these people. He began to wonder the same thing. Had he changed that much since his trip to Malaysia?"

"So this is a coven?" he heard Dempster saying as he stood behind Gail. "I count thirteen psychos."

"Now, please, detective, don't cause any trouble," advised Dr. Keld. "We all want this ceremony to be a success so we can go back to the city without any problems."

"I wouldn't think of causing any trouble, doctor," he replied with a grin. "I just think we should take the whole group back with us to the hospital."

"Yes, well, the others have yet to commit a crime," said the doctor.

"At least, any we are aware of," answered the detective. "I see they have no shortage of knives, anyway. You sure you want this so-called ceremony to take place, doctor?"

"Believe me, detective, it's the only way."

They would have continued talking, but Dr. Chen suddenly began banging upon his drum. He then began chanting words unknown to those listening, and sat down on the floor. Kolak walked over and sat down opposite him, folding his legs and placing his hands on his knees. The others in the coven, including Charlie Endor and Lil, sat down behind Kolak forming a semicircle as they listened intently to the shaman's chant.

"This should be interesting," mumbled Dempster with a smile, as he and Coggs stood off to the side. He then reached inside his jacket and touched the gun he had strapped around his waist.

Kolak glanced back at Dr. Chen, sitting silently with his eyes closed, his body appearing to have turned to stone.

"Hey, what's wrong with Chen?" asked the detective, as he began moving forward.

Dr. Keld stood up and extended his arm in front of him. "Don't worry, detective, he is falling into the trance," he said.

"But it looks as if something's wrong with him," argued the detective.

"It is the *lupa*," replied Dr. Keld. "He must achieve this state before proceeding to retrieve the tiger spirit."

Kolak saw the detective frown. He watched him as he shrugged his shoulders, and finally stepped backward, and then Kolak closed his eyes.

The shaman, hidden by a tiger skin, was chanting beneath the moonlight, the steady beat of his drum pulsing through the air. Then, suddenly, he halted his actions and fell into a trance. His face was without expression and his eyes were open, indifferent to everything around him. There was no horror, no fear, as his spirit slowly emerged . . .

Kolak felt the trance engulfing his own body, his will to resist fading like billowing smoke. He once again saw only the tiger, stepping softly through the dark Malaysian forest. He became one with the beast, snarling in the moonlit night, stalking the prey that would satiate his hunger, his terror, through the morning hours. He heard the roar of the beast echoing through his mind, the sympathetic twitches gripping his body, his muscles responding to the movements of the tiger as it rushed through the darkness of the forest . . . The *latah* . . .

Kolak opened his eyes, and saw the shaman still in the trancelike state known as the ecstasy. "He is of the *oobe*," some old Malay was saying. Kolak looked at the shaman and realized he had left his body and gone to the Netherworld to communicate with the gods, the tiger spirit having seized Kolak's soul . . .

He heard the steady beat of the drum pounding in his ears once again. He looked up and saw Dr. Chen sitting there striking the drum, the members of the coven sitting nearby. It was time for the ecstasy, and as Kolak waited for Dr. Chen to fall back into the trance, he noticed Lil holding the wax figure of the detective over a candle flame. The detective swayed in the light, and then finally collapsed in a nearby chair. "The *latah*," chanted Dr. Chen.

The shaman continued chanting, and then a halo of light appeared above his head. He was in the middle of the *lupa* and the very sight of it caused Kolak to tremble, bringing forth memories of the past, memories of Malaysia . . .

He saw the tiger rushing through the forest, following its prey. He stiffened as the tiger dashed onward. He was falling back into a tunnel, the light glistening in the distance. Ever falling, the tiger sprinting toward the light. Then he fell into sudden darkness, thrashing in the throes of a convulsive fit . . . and then all was silent once more . . .

Kolak opened his eyes. He thought he could see the tiger in the suffused light hovering above the shaman's head. It glowed for a moment and then sank down into the shaman's body . . .

A violent howl rumbled through the house, those inside startled by the fierce ululation seemingly emanating from Dr. Chen's open mouth. The sound jolted the detective to his feet, the sweat clinging to his forehead. He reached for his gun, pulled it from his holster, and held it in the air. Coggs also was holding a gun, waiting for the word to fire . . .

"Please, gentlemen, there's no need for those guns," urged Dr. Keld, standing up and holding his hands in the air. "Dr. Chen is simply in the midst of the ecstasy."

"But that noise, it's not human," Dempster replied.

"That's because it is the spirit inhabiting Mr. Kolak's soul, detective. And it is not of this world."

Kolak glanced at Dr. Chen, whose face was contorted, his lips moving out of sync with the sounds booming from inside. He could see the shaman's lips crease, his nose wrinkle, as he let out a resounding snarl. His eyes remained blank as the voice burst forth from muttering lips.

"Who has summoned me?" asked the deep, resonant voice.

Kolak could see the detectives looking at each other, still holding their guns, as the voice echoed across the room.

"I am not of your kind," the voice continued. "I am of the Underworld, although I have climbed the tree to the dwelling of the gods."

A sudden pain gripped Kolak's body.

"You have summoned me from another's soul," the voice thundered. "I was not done with that one. Allow me to return or your existence is surely in peril."

Dr. Chen remained motionless, his body rigid, as he sat cross-legged on the floor, his hands in a solemn clench. The others also sat and watched, mesmerized by the ghostly image projecting beyond Dr. Chen's head and body.

"I am of the great cat of Asia," the haunting voice bellowed across the room. "We have journeyed through the tall grass and the hidden waters that flow beyond the Temple of Kings. We have pursued the wild hog beneath the light of the midnight moon, and consumed the flesh of the forest dwellers, and have lived in peace among the deer and the buffalo and the shadows of the night. But, behold, there is one among us who disturbs the spirits of the forestland. He walks upright and does not discriminate among the dwellers of the Ancient Ruins. He calls himself, Man, and he wanders through the worlds of Those That Have Come Before—"

The apparition snarled at the words, causing the very foundation of the house to shudder.

"I have walked amongst these worlds and have seen the great monsters of the depths. I have come to know Man and his holy men and he has shown me the vast caverns of the Netherworld. We have climbed the Cosmic Tree and the Great Pillar and have seen the Upper World of the gods. These spirits sent me forth back into the forestlands, and there, I roamed amongst the trees and the vines. When Man visited my realm, he killed without reason, without worry, and so I appealed to the holy men and they placated and soothed me and promised me the soul of a Man. After much time, the shaman saw fit to give me this man—the man known as Kolak. I have become part of his soul, his other soul, and have wreaked revenge upon his fellow beings. And now you have summoned me once again to try to drive me back to the Netherworld. But I will stay, shaman. I will stay until this one known as Kolak is prepared to meet the gods—"

"No! You can't have him! He is mine!"

Kolak could hear Gail's voice, and then he slowly opened his eyes. "Flee while you still have the chance!" she was shouting. "Flee to the Netherworld!"

The apparition snarled once more, and then as a haunting howl burst from his lips, another ghastly phantom appeared. It was also in the form of a tiger, and as it let loose with a thunderous roar, the other spirit darted into the air and suddenly vanished behind one of the walls.

"But who has made him flee?" Gail wondered.

"It is the shaman, my dear," replied the doctor. "Don't worry, he has chased him back to the spirits."

Kolak clenched his teeth as another wave of pain rippled through his body. He felt himself falling back against the floor, and then he heard the voices of Charlie Endor and Lil. They were telling him to allow the tiger spirit back into his body.

"Is this some kind of trick?" the detective was now shouting. "Where did those images come from?"

He heard voices from behind and then the detective began to grumble. "So, this is one of your little tricks," he was saying. "I ought to arrest all of you for harboring a fugitive."

"We had nothing to do with any of this," he heard Lil say. "You better check with your shaman."

It was then Kolak felt another surge of pain and felt himself drifting through darkness.

The detective whirled around and glanced at Dr. Chen, who was still sitting motionless on the floor. He then ordered all the lights be turned on in the house and the members of the coven to leave the room. With Kolak lying on the floor moaning, Dempster approached one of the walls. He examined it for several moments, and then turned toward the doctor with a confused look on his face.

"Is he going to be all right?" he asked, pointing at Dr. Chen.

"I think so," answered Dr. Keld.

The detectives followed Dr. Keld toward the motionless shaman. They glanced at his face, pale and serene in the glaring light. Then Dr. Keld leaned forward to examine him, and without warning, Dr. Chen opened his eyes and blinked several times.

"Why, I don't believe it," said Dempster. "He was stiff as a board only a moment ago."

Dr. Chen's rigid body seemed to melt before their very eyes. He began to move his arms, and then stared up with a mysterious grin.

"I have been to the Yonder World," he finally whispered. "I led the tiger spirit to those of the Netherworld, the spirits of Erlen Khan."

"You've got to be kidding, doctor," the detective replied. "You mean to say those spirits actually exist?"

"Only if you choose to believe it is so," said Dr. Chen. "But I think you should ask Mr. Kolak to decide."

They turned toward Kolak. He was still lying on the floor, Gail kneeling over him with anxious concern.

"Is he all right?" the detective asked.

"I'm not sure," Gail answered in a worried voice. "He doesn't seem to be fully conscious. I think Dr. Keld better examine him."

The doctor knelt down and peered into Kolak's eyes. "I'd say he's still recovering from the strain of the whole affair," he finally said. "I think he'd better rest for a while."

"He can rest on the couch in the other room," said a voice from behind.

"Endor, I thought I ordered you to leave the room," replied Dempster. "This is no business of yours."

"But it surely is, detective," said Endor. "Roger is a friend of mine, and until he leaves this house, I will do everything I can to make sure he is all right. I know the rest of the coven agrees with me."

The detective looked up at Endor with a disapproving scowl. "This man is no longer your responsibility," he grumbled. "You understand? When he finally recovers, we're taking him with us and I don't want any interference from any of the members of this house. If anyone gets in our way, they will be arrested, and you can count on that."

He waited for Endor to reply, but none was forthcoming. Instead, Endor stood there staring at him with a vicious curl of the lips.

The detectives were helping lift Kolak from the ground when the lights suddenly flickered and the walls began to vibrate. Kolak listened as a haunting yowl echoed through the room. The walls began to rattle with greater intensity, and then the lights sizzled and went out completely leaving the room in total darkness. Gail screamed, and then the glowing image of a snarling tiger burst through the back wall and flitted about the room.

"Is this another trick?" wondered the detective, as the phantom darted toward them.

Before anyone could ponder the question, the image halted in the air and snarled once more.

"No, you can't have him, he belongs to me!" Gail shouted in the darkness.

The gleaming image hovered in the air, and then after a momentary silence, suddenly lunged for Kolak's body. He watched as it hurtled toward him, then halted in midair, another tiger spirit clinging to its flanks.

"Why, it must be Chen!" shouted Dr. Keld. "He must have gone back into a trance!"

The tiger spirit snarled as Chen's spirit hung on. Then, from behind the wall, another spirit emerged. It was in the shape of a hyena, with a short, doglike snout, and the outline of coarse, taut hair on the back and neck. The yellow-tinged glowing apparition charged toward Chen's spirit, opened its jaws, and bit down upon its leg. Chen's spirit shrieked in pain, releasing the tiger spirit it clung to.

"What the hell is going on?" murmured Dempster, fumbling for his gun. "Who is that other spirit that just attacked Chen?"

There was no reply as the tiger spirit whirled around and followed Chen's spirit toward the center of the room. The hyena spirit positioned itself on the other side of Chen's tiger, laughing derisively.

"Who has chosen to assist this one escape from the Underworld gods?" he could hear Chen saying from the other side of the room.

The hyena continued to laugh.

"Then I must take both of you back to the spirits!" Chen growled, the tiger image hovering in the air.

A tiger paw came slashing down upon the hyena before the words ceased to echo through the room. The other tiger spirit lunged forward, but Chen's tiger swiftly turned its head and tore into the tiger's head with its long, sharp shadowy teeth.

Kolak heard a deafening howl as the tiger spirit scrambled toward the back wall. The hyena, meanwhile, was no longer laughing. It sidled away from Chen's tiger yelping in pain. Chen let out a rumbling snarl and then charged toward the hyena. The hyena cowered, bracing itself for the attack. But just as Chen's tiger was about to pounce upon the cringing spirit, another spirit came dashing in from behind. It grabbed Chen's tiger in midair and then flung it away from the hyena.

"Now I will send you back to the gods!" howled the spirit. "Never to be seen again!"

Kolak watched as the spirit stood up on its hind legs, a massive phantom bear viciously snarling at Chen's tiger. He looked at the bear, and suddenly knew that Charlie Endor was somehow involved. As the bear spirit lunged toward the tiger, it grabbed it by the throat with one of its huge paws and hurled it across the room. He could hear Chen groan as the tiger landed beside the hyena, who proceeded to snatch it with its powerful jaws.

"They're going to kill him!" shouted Dr. Keld. Kolak could hear him stumbling in the darkness, trying to reach the groaning shaman.

Meanwhile, up above, Chen's spirit was in the midst of being mangled by the three other animal spirits. The hyena spirit and the other tiger continued to rip apart the glowing tiger image, while the massive bear spirit began dragging it back toward the wall. Then, suddenly, a scream echoed through the room in the direction of Dr. Chen.

The spirits burst out in scornful laughter as they sailed across the room and vanished behind the walls.

The lights suddenly flashed back on, and they could see Dr. Keld standing near the fallen shaman.

Kolak groaned, sat up, and rubbed his head.

"Is it over?" he asked, staring up at Gail.

Gail burst into tears, leaned over, and held him in her arms. "Yes, Roger, the spirits have finally gone," she sobbed. "You're safe now."

"There's only one problem," said Dr. Keld, walking toward them with a somber look upon his face.

"And what's that, doctor?" asked Kolak.

Dr. Keld halted in the middle of the room, staring at the others. "Dr. Chen is dead," he finally explained.

"It was the spirits," answered Kolak.

"Very strange spirits, I must admit," said the doctor. "But I don't think that was what killed Dr. Chen."

"Then what was it?" asked Detective Dempster, pulling out his gun.

"Well, see for yourself."

The two detectives walked over to the shaman, touched his shoulders, and he fell forward, revealing the hilt of a knife sticking out of his back.

"Why, he was murdered," Dempster said.

"If you will look at the blade of that knife, detective, you'll see it's bright silver—"

"And what does that mean, doctor?"

"Well, I fear it's the knife of the turnskin."

The detectives looked at Dr. Keld, who glanced back at Kolak, still sitting on the coven floor.

10

LIL'S WITCHCRAFT

THE WAX FIGURE BOILED AND bubbled as it hung above the flickering flame. Lil sat with a wicked smile on her face as she held the small charm above the melting candle. In the middle of the room, Detective Dempster stood wearing a feeble frown.

"All of these people are accessories to murder," he was saying to Coggs, the sweat glistening on his forehead. "I want you to call it in, and make sure you get an ambulance here as soon as possible."

Coggs nodded.

"And don't forget to ask them for backup," Dempster said, pulling a handkerchief from his pocket.

Coggs hurried for the door.

"Tell them this is an emergency," Dempster shouted.

He watched as Coggs opened the door and dashed outside. He then turned toward the members of the coven and paused for a moment. A cackling laugh tittered in the air.

"Go ahead and laugh now," he grumbled. "But very soon every one of you is going to be laughing in prison."

"You have no evidence of our involvement in anyone's murder," said Charlie Endor, stepping forward.

"That's what you think," snapped the detective. "Wait until we analyze that knife. Anyway, I'll get all of you on harboring a fugitive."

There was silence for a moment, and then Lil stood up, and began walking toward him. "Now can't we forget all this foolishness?" she said with a sly grin.

"There's nothing foolish about any of this," the detective replied. "And what's that you're holding in your hand?"

"Why this, detective? It's only a figure made of wax."

Lil approached one of the tables and placed the figure down.

"Why are you melting it?"

"You see, this figure represents an enemy of mine and I am gradually destroying it," she said. "And when it is finally completely destroyed, I imagine so will my enemy."

"And who is this enemy?" asked the detective, patting his forehead with his handkerchief.

Lil smiled. "Why, it happens to be you, detective," she finally said.

"Me?" he said with disdain.

"A pretty good likeness, wouldn't you say?"

"Do you actually expect me to believe that that image has any relation to my emotional bearing?"

"I would say so, detective."

The detective sneered. "I always thought you people were a bunch of psychos," he said. "Maybe if you're lucky, you'll all be assigned to the same mental ward."

"Then why are you feeling so weak, detective?"

"I feel fine," the detective replied. "Now why don't you take your doll and sit back down."

"But I'm going to continue to walk out that door—"

"Sit down, you freak!"

"There's nothing you can do about it, detective—"

"I'll use this gun if I have to—"

"But you have no use for that gun. You see, you're feeling tired and you're about to fall asleep."

The detective held the handkerchief to his forehead, a strange fever overtaking his brain. It was as if he hadn't slept for days, his eyelids feeling thick and ready to close.

"Get back over—"

Before the detective could finish the words, Lil produced a small knife and began cutting underneath the figure's head. When it finally toppled over, she turned and looked at the detective. He was slowly slumping to the ground, his eyes half-closed, as the sweat spilled across his forehead. She watched as he slowly sunk to the floor, rolled over, and finally fainted.

"What did you do to him?" shouted Gail, as she hurried to his side. She knelt down, attempting to determine whether he was still breathing.

"Nothing that won't wear off eventually," said Lil. "And now I'm afraid all of us must be leaving."

She looked at Charlie Endor and the other members of the coven and smiled. They proceeded to saunter across the floor, staring down at the fallen detective. Then Lil turned to Kolak, who was still sitting on the floor attempting to ascertain whether the tiger spirit still inhabited his mind.

"You're coming with us, aren't you, Mr. Kolak?" she asked.

"I'm not sure," he mumbled.

Upon hearing the words, Gail stood up and hurried toward him. "Oh, you mustn't leave, Roger," she implored. "There's hope for you now. The spirits are gone."

"But how can you be sure?"

"Dr. Chen sacrificed his life," she said. "Surely, you're not thinking of leaving me again—"

"But where would we go?"

"I'm afraid I'd have to take you back to the hospital," said Dr. Keld, making his way across the room. "You see, even if the spirits are gone, you are going to need a lot of rest and rehabilitation before you can lead a normal life again—"

"The hospital? But I'll never go back there—"

"I'm afraid I must insist," said Dr. Keld. "There's still the matter of killing all those people."

"But you saw for yourself what caused Roger to kill," argued Gail. "It was those spirits—"

"Yes, my dear, but who is going to believe any of it? Do you think the detectives are going to say they saw those spirits? I regret to say they will not, and now Dr. Chen is dead, a knife sticking in his back. There's no one except you and I, and I will not try to explain it to my colleagues until we find out who that knife belongs to."

"Then what choice does Roger have?"

"None at all, I'm afraid. I think his only chance is to run and to keep running until he fades from our memories. I'll do my best to convince the authorities that he escaped without leaving us any idea where he was headed. Maybe that way they'll finally forget about him—"

Gail turned toward Kolak and began to weep. "Oh, Roger, where will you go? Who will make sure that you're all right?"

"I don't know," he muttered. "But I think the doctor is right. As long as there's no proof of any of this happening, no one with any authority will believe us."

She bent down, cradled his head in her arms, and continued to cry. "Don't worry, darling, we'll find a way to prove it to them," she said. "And then you'll be free again and can come back to me, and maybe, we'll learn how to be happy again just like before."

"If only I can believe that," he replied.

"But you must, Roger. You must continue to hope. You must continue to believe that everything will work out just as though we had planned it that way—"

Kolak looked down. "You're the only reason for me to want to go on living," he finally said. "Without the possibility of being in your arms again, what hope would there be for me?"

"Then listen to the doctor, Roger. Hide somewhere and don't get caught until we straighten this whole thing out."

"And how about you, Gail? How long before you decide to forget?"

"Oh, don't talk like that," she gushed. "You know if it only could be like before, I would be with you until the end of time. But things have changed, and we both must accept that until the situation can be corrected."

"Yes, you're right, of course," he replied. He stood up, glanced at the detective and Dr. Chen, and then looked back into her eyes. "Are you going to be all right?" he asked.

She nodded. "But you must go quickly, Roger, before the police arrive," she said.

He looked at her, leaned forward, and kissed her. She held him for a moment, wrapped her arms around him, and kissed him again. Then she watched as he staggered across the room, opened the back door, and hurried outside into the dark, blue night.

"You realize the tiger spirit hasn't left his body," said Lil, still standing nearby. "It's only a matter of time before he changes again."

"And how could you know that?" replied Gail. "As far as I'm concerned, Dr. Chen was successful in removing it from his soul, and then it fled back to the Netherworld."

"You really don't believe in all of this magic nonsense, do you, my dear?"

"As long as Roger believes in it, that's all I care about."

Lil began to laugh, a high-pitched, shrieking cackle, and walked toward the fallen detective.

"And what about you, detective, surely you believe."

Dempster, beginning to regain his senses, frowned at the remark.

"And what about you, doctor, you still have your doubts?"

Dr. Keld looked at her and slowly nodded. "You see, I know witchcraft is only an illusion," he whispered. "You people have no power to defy God and Nature."

"Is that so, doctor? And how about it if I demonstrated to you how much you really don't know."

"Absurd," the doctor replied.

"Really now," laughed Lil. She glared at them, then began to tremble, her arms shaking violently, her head suddenly thickening, melting, distorting, until the short snout appeared, and coarse fur began sprouting across her face.

Gail screamed, covered her eyes, and then peered between her fingers at the creature before her. She immediately recognized it as the hyena, the spirit that helped to mangle Dr. Chen's tiger spirit.

"So it was you," she said, gasping in terror.

The creature shook its head and began laughing with scorn.

Gail slowly moved backwards toward the doctor and detective, an uncontrollable shiver rushing through her body.

"I should kill all of you now!" the creature hissed. It leaned forward, baring its long, razor-sharp teeth and began cackling once again.

Dempster sat up, squinted at the creature, and tried to convince himself what he was seeing was actually real. The doctor, meanwhile, grabbed Gail, put his arms around her, and stepped backwards behind the detective.

"So, she too, suffers from pathological lycanthropy," he muttered. "Quite incredible."

They watched as the beast moved forward, the tapered claws jutting from the outstretched hands. Charlie Endor and the members of the coven watched with evil grins.

"Maybe you should spare the girl," he finally said.

The beast looked at him and hissed, and then erupted into another jarring cackle.

"Really, Lil, you know Roger seems to like her."

The beast snarled at the remark, and leaned forward. It was about to lunge for the detective when the sound of sirens suddenly throbbed through the air.

"The police," said Charlie Endor. "We'd better get going."

The beast snarled, paused for a moment, and then wheeled around, stomping across the room. They watched as it reached the back door, and rushed outside. The other members of the coven soon followed.

Gail looked at Dr. Keld with fear and astonishment, and he returned the glance with a solemn nod. Dempster, meanwhile, was busy staring at the headless wax figure Lil had left upon the table. He winced for a moment, still contemplating all that occurred, when the door flew open and several police officers hurried inside.

Darkness filled the sky, the rain having drifted to the east, as Kolak stumbled his way through the gloomy landscape. He had convinced himself that he should proceed northward, hoping someone or something would help him decide what to do next. Without the ability to transform any longer, there wasn't any reason to ever go back to the coven. He thought about Gail, the genuine concern etched upon her face, and wondered if he would ever really see her again. Theirs had been a surprisingly sturdy love, and as he shuffled through the shadows of the night, he couldn't help feeling that it was about to vanish within the fading echoes of time.

He wandered through the trees and the cool air until a feeling of weariness began to overwhelm him. He was still trying to recover from the trauma of the evening and all that had occurred the past few days, when he decided to sit down on the moist ground for a few moments. As he lay back amid the gentle silence, his thoughts drifted once more toward Gail. How pleased he was that she had supported him during these difficult days, still offering her love with generous care, still rendering words filled with hope and reassurance. How he still loved her, wanted to be with her all the time, and hear her serene voice remind him of the soft glow of moonlight . . .

Kolak stared up into the night sky. The clouds had passed, the glistening stars peering through the darkness. Just what had he learned in those months spent in Malaysia? A creature haunted by superstition, placing himself above Nature and a slave to the heavens. He had studied the life of those people, their societal structure and magic, and had found even a civilized being was susceptible to its ancient precepts. But if Gail was correct, there was still a chance to overcome these primitive directives, still time to seek spiritual redemption . . .

Gail . . . she had always been his key to optimism. Their love had been founded upon mutual understanding, intellectual as well as emotional, and it had grown from its innocent beginnings. She had come to understand his philosophical outlook, his hopes, his dreams, his goals, and even his disappointments, and he had come to understand hers. They were swept away by the passion of the moment and the prospects of the future, and eventually, agreed that their desires and visions intersected and that a life together might actually attain some meaning and lead to some sort of mutual spiritual awakening. Yes, it was possible. They would remain optimistic about the human potential . . .

"There really is no reason to fear," she had said as they stood there in Times Square amid the jostling crowd waiting for the moment when the world would know whether the end had come, whether the new millennium would bring just another uneventful day or the apocalypse itself as foretold in the Book of Revelation. "Human beings have issued dark prophecies since the beginning of time, whether it be an eclipse or the passing of a comet."

"Yes, and things have always gone on just as before," he replied. "I mean, people even disagree when the millennium begins. For some, it's not for another year, for others, it doesn't start for another thirty-three years, the anniversary of Jesus' death. And for others, it's not even the same year because they use different calendars."

"So, I guess we should just enjoy the moment while we can," she said. "Whatever moment it may be."

They stood there smiling at each other, buried in each other's arms, the cold air fading in puffs of frozen breath, waiting as the shadow of time swept across the planet. Then they heard it had reached Australia, then on to the Great Pyramid at Giza, then fell upon Rome and moved onward across the Eiffel Tower and Greenwich, England. The planet remained in its orbit, continued to spin in its journey around the Sun, and then the moment descended upon New York City, and they rejoiced, flinging confetti into the air, and shouting toward the heavens.

"You see?" she gushed. "Everything is as it was before. Things can only get better now. We have nothing to fear but our own nightmares."

He thought about the gleam in her eyes, the undeniable exultation in her voice, as the shadow swept by them and onward toward the Pacific. The human race had survived its own perilous fears, the ancient monoliths and ruins still throwing shadows at the night . . .

The night. He felt a chill dance through his body and looked up at the gleaming stars. Gail had been right, as always. Things had gotten better as the days slowly drifted by. Their appreciation for each other only grew, and with it, his reputation as an anthropologist who was willing to collect empirical data by living among the diverse cultures of the world. He had been inspired by Gail's optimism, and had come to believe it was possible to find the answers he was seeking. He would attempt to find out how the human being developed, evolved, and how he had adapted his societies through the ages. And then came the opportunity to go to Malaysia . . .

"I'll wait for you," she had said as he prepared for the long trip ahead. "Our love will sustain us until you return."

"And if I find what I'm looking for, such as the keys to culture and personality, then we can finally get married and live in the splendor you deserve," he had replied.

"I'm planning to be your partner through life with or without splendor," she said. "I'll always believe in you no matter what happens in Malaysia."

Then the time finally came, and he looked her in the eyes, and attempted to store in his mind and heart everything about her.

"I'll be waiting for you," she said with tears running down her cheeks. "Oh, Roger, make sure nothing happens to destroy everything we've worked so hard to build."

He kept staring at her, hoping her image would sustain him during the long days ahead, and then he turned and walked away . . .

The image of her standing there, the tears rolling down her soft skin, still remained etched in his mind. She remained waiting until his return. His return. It was soon after his return that he discovered the curse had remained with him. The laughter of the Malays echoed through his mind. But the belief that the curse, the *latah*, could be broken also remained. After all, he was a scientific man, someone who had spent his life studying the faults and vices of the human race . . . He remembered that September morning when the World Trade Center towers came crashing down. The evil and memories rushed through his mind. It was almost as if a higher being had demonstrated to him the true nature of evil in the world, and that overcoming it was a task for only the strongest. And there was Gail once again, ready to support him with love and optimism.

"You see, you're not the only one who feels as if some sort of great evil has infected his life," she was saying. "There are thousands, millions, who feel exactly the same way."

"Yes, but I'm a part of this evil," he had replied. "I know you don't really understand what I'm talking about, but I feel this evil has invaded my body, my inner soul."

"It may be anthrax or the ebola virus or something like that, Roger. This terrorism scare has everyone thinking they've been infected with some sort of evil."

"This is an evil that didn't come from any anthrax powder. It was evil buried deep within my soul and the only thing I can do is try to find its origin."

"But you're not really sure," she had replied. "It could be just a virus you picked up. Oh, please, let a doctor check you out, Roger. It could be something fatal if not taken care of."

He only wished it had been fatal. But this was no virus, no anthrax poisoning, it was something much worse. It was as if he had a premonition of a curse, something like a disease that he would have to live with for who knows how long. It was said that once the curse was consummated, it could never be undone or reversed. Only the shaman who had fixed the curse could possibly exorcise the demon from the infected man's soul and lead it back to the Netherworld. In the meantime, the one who was cursed was damned to lust for human blood and take whatever human he could find . . . He wondered if Gail knew just what kind of danger had become a part of her life. He thought about the Malays, and then his parents trying to convince him to pursue a different career. In all those years, they never really believed in his ability to study the human beast . . .

"Where is it going to get you?" his father demanded. "Studying all these other people, all these other cultures? Just what in the hell are you looking for? That human beings are primitive in their wants and demands? That we came from some killer beast that had refined itself through the centuries with religion, culture and technology? Well, hell, I can tell you that right now. And some of the people I deal with are not that far removed. They still have the human beast lurking inside."

"But only by scientific study can we ascertain what to do about it," he had explained. "I mean, through science, we can find a way to eradicate the beast forever."

"Not very likely," his father had replied. "Some of these traits and quirks of the human soul run deep down into the human personality. Why, it would take someone years to discover all the things that cause a person to act the way he does. I mean, my God, I don't fully understand all the things I do myself. You want to go understand others?"

He had nodded at the remark, and at the time, still felt optimistic about eventually finding the answer. His father didn't understand. Never did. He was a businessman whose only cares had been money and deals. He never cared to really examine the true nature of the creature he was dealing with . . .

The human beast. He had come to disregard Nature in the name of money and technology, but the beast was still there buried deep inside. There was evidence of it in personal relations and world events. And now he had been forced to confront the beast within himself. It had scared him how ferocious the beast could be. It was a bloodthirsty killer. And he feared that in some way it was a part of all of us, a distasteful part of our past, our history, and had become part of our disposition. He thought about the true nature of the beast. He had seen it in Malaysia, but thought he was above such primitive weaknesses. But he wanted to understand, wanted to pinpoint the beast, and bring it back alive in all its savage glory . . .

The Malays sat there watching, chanting and banging, as he held the wooden cup in his hands and began drinking the mixture of herbs.

The salve had been applied to his body and around his waist he wore a tiger pelt. Amid the loud moaning and screaming, he felt as if the temperature had suddenly dropped and a form had appeared in the darkness. It was part-human, part-beast and he knew he had found what he had desperately been looking for . . .

He glanced up at the moon, glowing in the distant sky. A cold sweat had overtaken his body, his mind. He tried to ignore it, and then a spasm rippled through his limbs, and he knew the awful past was upon him. He leaned back, fell into a convulsive fit, and the spirit of the tiger began to emerge. He groaned, tried to scream, but the sound was lost within a guttural snarl. He could see the tiger once again racing through the Malaysian forest, the fierce growl vibrating through his entire body. It enveloped his mind, his soul, and then the horrible transformation began. His muscles stiffened and began to pulse, and he felt himself changing, distorting. He could feel his clothes bursting apart at the seams, and then he glanced up and noticed the moon enveloped in a yellow tinge. He had become the tiger once more, and as he stood up he could feel the overwhelming desire for human flesh and the dank smell of human blood surging through his mind and senses . . .

He carefully moved forward, the gracefulness of the cat within him, the stealthy movements of the hunter imbuing every step. He could hear voices in the distance, the shouting of human beings beyond the silhouetted trees. A shot suddenly crackled through the air, the groan of the victim piercing the night. He hurried into the darkness, could see a huge figure stumbling to the ground. As he edged closer, he could see it was an enormous bear gurgling in agony. He moved closer, and realized it was Charlie Endor.

Kolak dashed toward the fallen figure as the human voices echoed through the night air. He stood there trying to suppress his snarling, trying to control his other soul, and leaned forward, wondering what he should do, what he could do in his present state.

"Roger?" grunted the wounded bear. "Hide me before they find us. Hurry, there's not much time."

Kolak bent down, and without thinking, wrapped the creature's arm around his neck and began pulling him into the shadows. There was still shouting nearby, the voices of the hunters, and Kolak crouched down beside the wounded beast and let out a subdued hiss.

"Quiet, Roger," the beast moaned.

Kolak could hear the voices getting closer. A thought suddenly emerged in his head that told him he mustn't be caught in the form of the tiger. He didn't know where the thought had come from, or why it was resounding through his mind, but he knew it was right. He wondered if he had the power to overcome the tiger spirit, and then Kolak closed his eyes, and slowly fell asleep beside the wounded beast.

11

THE INJURED BEAR

"OVER HERE!" SHOUTED A POLICE officer, weaving his way through the darkness and the sprawling vegetation. "I think I wounded him!"

The other officers followed him into the maze of shadows, clutching guns that glinted in the soft moonlight. They searched the grounds for several moments, and then they stopped, trying to decide in which direction to proceed.

"Are you sure you hit it?" asked one of the officers, sifting through the dim terrain. "I mean, maybe you just scared it. It's probably headed back to the hills."

"No, I definitely hit him!" shouted back the officer. "I heard him groaning in pain. It was the biggest damned bear I had ever seen in this area."

"All I saw was a dark shadow," replied the other officer. "But I did hear him growling, there's no doubt of that."

The officers peered between the bushes, and stepped around the thick trees, listening for any sounds that might be carried upon the cool wind. But there was only silence, the soft breeze swaying amid the taut limbs. They glanced behind them and could see a woman and an older man hurrying through the darkness.

"Please be careful, officers," implored Dr. Keld. "These people engage in witchcraft. There's no telling what they may do to place us in a compromising position."

"Then you think that bear was the result of witchcraft, doctor?" asked one of the officers.

"I did not say that," replied the doctor. "Only that you should be careful until those people are apprehended."

"Well, careful or not, we still have to locate that bear," said an officer. "We can't just let it roam around among a populated area."

"But it might not be just a bear," said Gail. "I mean, we've already seen one of them turn into an animal. Roger was also capable of this feat, and I fear there might be others."

"You telling us what we saw may have been a human being?"

"It just might well have been," explained Gail. "Some of them suffer from a very serious disease."

"And this disease causes them to turn into animals?" asked the officer incredulously.

"She's telling the truth, officer," interjected Dr. Keld. "It's called pathological lycanthropy, and we saw an absolute display of it back at the house. One of them escaped from my hospital—"

"What I saw was no maniac, doctor, but a large and quite normal bear," answered the officer who had fired his gun. "They sometimes stray from the wooded hills in search of food."

"But how can you be sure?"

"I know a bear when I see one, doctor. Now you can tell us anything you want about those psychos running around, but there's no doubt in mind that what I shot at was a bear."

The officer looked at the others and then continued searching. Gail watched them as they slowly advanced into the darkness. She stood there, deciding whether to follow them, when she heard a voice whisper her name.

"Gail."

She turned, peered into the dim shadows, and heard the voice once again.

"Gail, over here."

She moved slowly in the direction she thought the voice was coming from, and then suddenly saw a shadow of a man leaning out from behind a bush.

"Roger, is that you?" she whispered back.

"Hurry, Charlie's injured."

She approached the bush and knelt down, staring into the eyes of the man she once planned to marry. She put her arms around him, sunk into his arms, and then kissed him on the cheek. Then she noticed Charlie Endor sprawled upon the ground beside them.

"Is he hurt?" she asked.

"He needs medical attention," Kolak replied. "You'd better get the doctor."

She leaned back, held his hand for a moment, and then noticed his torn clothing. "Did the bear attack you too, Roger?" she gasped.

"I had to help Charlie," he replied. "Go and get the doctor."

She nodded, glanced into his eyes, and stood up. "You wait there, Roger," she said. "Maybe you don't have to keep running."

She stepped into the darkness as Kolak waited beside Charlie Endor.

"Do you know what you're doing, Roger?" he groaned.

"They don't know who or what you are, Charlie," he whispered back. "They'll think a bear attacked us. Look at our clothes, they won't think to question it."

"Roger," Charlie whispered. "I told you that you would learn to control your other soul."

Kolak looked at him and nodded. "Well, I had a pretty damn good teacher," he replied.

Endor smiled, and then Gail stepped back into the shadows, Dr. Keld hurrying close behind.

"Kolak, what happened to both of you?" asked the doctor.

"It was the bear, he attacked us."

"Are you sure that was a real bear?" the doctor asked.

"It was I who turned into a tiger," answered Kolak. "That is, until Dr. Chen removed the spirit."

Dr. Keld stared down at the blood oozing across the front of Charlie Endor's shirt. He shook his head and turned toward Kolak.

"Well, I won't be able to examine him here," he finally said. "We've got to carry him back to the cars and get him to a hospital. I think we're going to need some police officers to help us."

They watched him as he turned and began shouting into the darkness. "We've got a man down!" he said. "We need some help, officers!"

After a few moments, three police officers approached. "What seems to be the problem, doctor?" one of them asked.

"One of the people from the house was attacked by the bear," he replied.

"What's the extent of the injuries?"

"I won't know until I get him into the light. This man over here was also attacked."

The officers peered into the shadows. "What man?" one of them finally asked.

Dr. Keld turned around. Kolak was gone.

The figure dashed across the landscape, past the bushes and trees, toward the old Victorian house. He stumbled at the back door, and slipped inside. He stepped across the floor, into the room with the pentagram, and up onto the altar. He glanced at the athame, the double-bladed knife used in witchcraft, sitting on the table, the censor, the container used for the burning of incense, and the chalice, and then grabbed the two books lying beside them.

He opened one of the books and began turning the pages. He skimmed through the many rites and incantations, still searching for anything pertaining to healing. WIND SCRYING, THE ETHERIC AURA, THE ASTRAL AURA, MAGIC CIRCLE . . . He suddenly stopped at one of the pages entitled, Spells to Remove a Curse.

He stared at the page, and began reading. Two candles, eight inches long, one black, one white . . . A bag of charcoal . . . The Knight of Swords tarot card . . . Dig a hole twelve inches deep . . . Fill the hole with the charcoal . . . Seven circles with a knife around the white candle . . . Seven around the black candle . . . Repeat the words, 'creo del macres ete prestwer' . . .

He stopped reading, tore the page from the book, folded it and placed it inside one of his pockets, and continued flipping through the pages.

"Roger?" a voice whispered.

Kolak glanced up, saw Gail standing near the altar, and jumped back. He closed the book he was reading, and quickly placed it back upon the table.

"What is that book?" asked Gail.

"N-Nothing," stammered Kolak. "Silly old magic books."

"Then why were you looking at them?"

"I thought I might be able to help Charlie."

"I can't believe that there is anything in those books that could help heal Charlie's wounds," she said.

"But there are, Gail. There are all kinds of spells and rituals and healing procedures."

Gail frowned. "I thought when Dr. Chen died you would forget all about spirits and spells and magic," she said. "Oh, Roger, don't you see how unhealthy all of this is? I mean, you're supposed to have a scientific mind. How can you allow yourself to believe in all this primitive superstition?"

". . . But it's happened again, Gail," he replied. "I don't know how or why, but I felt the convulsions again, and then I began to transform—"

"Oh, Roger, it's all just psychological—"

"No, Gail, I felt the spasms, and then the physical changes."

Gail bowed her head and began to cry. "Then I guess you'll never be cured of this disease, this curse," she sobbed. "I hoped I could make you understand, convince you that you were being deceived, but I see you've decided to hang on to these beliefs, these misconceptions."

"But look, Gail, there's still a chance." He pulled the piece of paper from his pocket, unfolded it, and showed it to her.

"You believe in this spell?" she asked.

"Why not? If only you could have seen me for yourself—"

"Then it was you the police were shooting at."

Kolak shook his head. "They never saw me," he said. "It was Charlie they were shooting at."

"You mean to say—"

"Yes, Charlie was the bear."

She gasped. "Then Dr. Keld and those police officers are in danger," she said. "And Roger you helped him."

"I didn't know what else to do. Charlie's injured, I don't think he'll transform again."

"Does it matter if he does or not?" she replied. "He's a killer all the same."

"But he's injured—"

Before Kolak could finish, Gail turned and ran from the room. "We must warn them," she said.

He watched her hurry for the front door, and then followed in silence.

They carried Charlie Endor to one of the police cars, opened the door, and Dr. Keld began to examine the injured man in the glowing light.

"A bullet wound," the doctor exclaimed. "Then it was you—"

Charlie Endor began to laugh, a low, terrifying laugh filled with hatred and disdain.

"Yes, doctor," he finally said. "It was I."

Dr. Keld jumped backward, tried to run, but Endor's hands were already grasping his neck. The police officers standing nearby reached for their guns, but Endor suddenly stepped back and swung his arm, knocking them to the ground. He then turned back toward Dr. Keld.

"Now watch, doctor," he said. "I think this is something for your medical books."

Dr. Keld tried to run once again, but Endor caught him and wrapped his hands around his neck. Then, suddenly, Endor's head slid up his spine, and his shoulders broadened, his hands thickened. Dr. Keld gasped for breath, stared up into the distorting face and tried to scream. He could see the hair beginning to grow at a rapid pace on Endor's hands and face. There was a sudden snarl, a deep rolling rumble, and then Dr. Keld trembled as the rapier fangs glistened in the moonlight. He stared into the beast's eyes, gleaming with malignity. Then Endor's nose began to elongate, finally forming a snout, and the bear appeared.

"Show's over, doctor," the beast growled.

Dr. Keld was still trembling as the beast's grip became tighter, the brutish hands wringing the life from his dangling body. He glanced up at the malevolent eyes with a bewildered look on his face and then suddenly went limp, his neck broken by the ferocious clench.

The police officers, watching the fierce display, edged backwards, their eyes agape in mortal fear. They gazed at the beast as he let go of Dr. Keld, his body crumbling silently to the damp ground, and felt the paralysis of terror wash over them.

The beast snarled, and then staggered toward them, his outstretched hands ending in long, sharp claws.

"But how the hell is it possible?" mumbled one of the officers, as the beast sneered with contempt.

One of the officers, suddenly reacting to the awesome threat, reached for his gun, and in that moment, the beast was upon him. There was a groaning shout of surprise and pain as the beast lifted him off the ground, and savagely sunk his teeth into his throat. With blood gushing from the wound, the beast picked him up over his head and hurled him to the ground. The officer hit the ground with a thud, and then spun to a halt, the blood spilling across the dank pavement.

The beast growled, turned toward another one of the officers, and lunged at him. The officer's eyes jumped open, he staggered backwards, and then turned and dashed down the street. Another officer, standing behind the creature, steadied himself holding his gun out in front of him and fired a shot. The bullet tore into the creature's hindquarter and a piercing howl echoed in the misty air.

Blood oozed from the beast's matted hair as he spun around and charged at the stunned officer. With a swipe of the beast's claws, the officer fell hard against the pavement. Then, with a terrific snarl, the creature bent down and, with one wrenching motion, tore the officer's arm from his socket.

Gail and Kolak stood on the front porch of the old Victorian house watching as Charlie Endor mangled the officer's arm. Gail gasped in disgust, and then Kolak stepped forward toward the street.

"Charlie!" he shouted. "Now you have killed!"

The beast glanced at him, snarled with disdain, and then proceeded to sink his fangs into the officer's arm, ripping a chunk of flesh from the bloodied limb.

'They're going to hunt us down until all of us are dead, Charlie!" shouted Kolak. "Don't you realize that?"

Endor sneered. "Do you think I really care, you foolish coward," he hissed back. "We must fight them whether we want to or not. And what about you, Kolak, what do you choose to do?"

Kolak glanced back at Gail, standing in shock and fear, and then bowed his head. Endor sneered once again, finally hurling the arm at Kolak.

"So you think you and your darling are going to escape?" he thundered.

Kolak didn't hear the words. The severed arm landed at his feet, causing him to fall backwards upon the damp pavement. Endor laughed, a hideous cackle, and then lumbered toward Gail, his eyes flashing through the darkness.

"So you think you can just leave us?" gabbled the beast.

Kolak heard Gail scream, and then the convulsions rippled through his body, and he felt his body begin to change. Gail watched for a moment, could see the beast shuffling toward her and Kolak writhing on the pavement slowly transforming into the tiger, and began to scream once again.

"What's the matter, my dear?" mocked Endor, as he made his way across the street.

As he reached Gail, there was a loud grumbling, the gnashing of teeth, and then a snarling figure leaped into the air and upon Endor's back. Endor howled in pain, and Gail stumbled backwards in horror and disbelief.

The enormous bear twisted his body until finally grabbing the growling tiger, lifting him off his back and throwing him into the street. The tiger landed on his feet, snarled once again, and flung himself back toward the howling beast.

As the fight continued, Gail hurried toward one of the police cars, noticing Detective Dempster sitting inside. She raised her hand, and as she reached the door, the detective leaned over and opened it.

"Are you all right, Miss?" he asked, sliding over and allowing her to climb into the front seat.

She nodded, began to sob, and fell into his arms. "Then it's all true," she said. "Roger does actually become the tiger."

"A living nightmare is more like it," replied the detective. "I've already radioed for more officers."

She peered through the windshield, into the darkness, but could see no sign of either creature. "Well, at least, they've gone," she finally said. "I hope Roger isn't injured."

A bitter smile creased the detective's face. "That isn't Roger or any other human being," he said. "They're some kind of demons. Did you see how that woman changed into that hyena? Nothing like that is possible in this world—"

"But Dr. Keld said it was a result of a disease—"

"There's no disease like that I ever heard of," Dempster said. "Why, they get shot and only get angrier. How are we supposed to stop them?" His words fell off into an incoherent mumbling.

"But the doctor said you have to burn them to kill the demonic soul," she said. "That seems to be the only way." She paused for a moment and began to shake her head. "Poor Dr. Keld," she murmured.

"The doctor told me the same thing," frowned Dempster. "That's why we brought along a can of gasoline. Just in case."

"Gasoline?" repeated Gail. "Why, that's wonderful. But how can we actually use it on another human being—"

"They're not human beings, I tell you," rejoined the detective. "Besides, it's the only possible way to stop them. You heard the doctor yourself, silver bullets or fire. Well, I have no idea where we can obtain silver bullets, so fire will have to do."

"But the idea of setting these beings on fire—"

"Did you see what that bear creature did to those officers and the doctor? And regular bullets don't seem to harm them."

They fell silent for a moment, both of them staring through the windshield, searching for the creatures.

"Now I'll go out and get the gasoline from the trunk," he said. "If you see anything, shout real loud so I can hear you."

Gail nodded, and then Dempster slowly opened the door and slipped outside. She sat there, nervously peering through the window, and then, several moments later, the detective reappeared holding a red and yellow gallon can.

"This should be enough," he said, sliding back into the car. "Maybe if we kill one, the others will surrender."

Gail was about to reply when there was a knocking on the car window. It was Detective Coggs and he was standing beside a small female with black hair.

"Good work, detective," greeted Dempster, opening the car door. "I see you captured one of the witches—"

"Her name is Jessie," Coggs replied. "She was walking through the woods."

They opened the rear door, and Jessie slid inside. Dempster then shifted toward Gail, and Coggs sat down behind the steering wheel.

"What've you got there, detective?" asked Coggs.

"Gasoline," Dempster replied. "It's the only way to stop these creatures."

"You're not planning to burn any of them, are you?" asked Jessie with concern.

"Well, we were thinking about it," Dempster snorted. "Is there any other way to destroy them?"

"Destroy them?" repeated Jessie. "But they're such powerful and vibrant beings. How can you even consider destroying them?"

"Is murder a good enough reason?" Dempster retorted. "Did you see what your vibrant friends did to the doctors, as well as those police officers? Well, we can't have them rampaging through the countryside. We have no choice but to destroy them."

"But it was all supposed to be about Nature," Jessie said. "We were only looking to utilize its powers."

"But don't you see?" replied Gail. "All you've succeeded in doing is to pervert those powers."

There was silence for a moment, and then they could hear the sirens screaming in the night. Moments later, the ambulance and police cars pulled up to the curb, and in the bright flashing lights, they began collecting the bodies.

"Do you know who's responsible for all this?" asked one of the officers.

Dempster nodded his head, and grimaced. "It was them," he finally said.

"Them?" repeated the startled officer.

The detective looked down at the puddles of blood, the lights glowing in deep reflections. He then walked back to the police car, opened the door, and grabbed the can of gasoline.

"It's the only way, isn't it, Jessie?" he asked the young woman in the back seat.

She looked at him. "It'll destroy their souls forever," she cried. "Don't you understand?"

The detective nodded, and carrying the red can, slowly walked back toward the glaring lights.

Jessie hung her head and began to sob, the tears rolling down her cheeks and vanishing into the darkness below.

12

DEATH

THE MALAYS WERE GRINNING. THEY were standing over the dead body and chanting their approval in wild hoots and shrieks. He had listened to their cries, felt the utter shame inside him, and slowly walked back through the Malaysian forest. "The *latah* is strong within you," he remembered the shaman saying, his arms raised toward the heavens . . .

That was the first time he had killed. He had seen the tiger spirit within his soul, his muscles twitching in concert with the stalking beast. He had followed the creature through the ragged vegetation, exploring his world, duplicating his actions as he weaved his way into the shadows. Then he had felt the stiffening of his muscles, the terrifying scream of death, and had realized he must obey the savage voice inside him . . .

Kolak thought about the Malays and the fierce snarl of the tiger as he stared down at Charlie Endor's body. He had almost killed again, and once again, a feeling of remorse swirled inside his soul. He knew he was lucky to still be alive. Endor, however, had been severely weakened by the bullets that had torn through his body. He realized Endor was only following the spirit that had seized his soul, the thirst for murder inescapable, inexorable. He would kill, and continue killing, until he was swallowed by the darkness and then possibly awakened once again in the glimmer of the morning light . . .

Kolak looked down at Endor's motionless body. He had emerged victorious, and now in control of his human soul, he pondered in which direction he should proceed. He glanced up at the hunched row of hills in the distance, wondering if he should vanish in the enveloping darkness, and try to make his way north . . . He thought about it for a moment, and then turned back toward the old Victorian house. Gail was still there, he was sure of it. But she had finally seen him transform into the tiger and he wondered if that would change everything forever. Could she still love him after seeing what he had become, what evil lurked within his soul? He stood thinking about what her reaction might be, and then decided she was still his only chance to live again. What meaning did his existence have if she was not a part of it? What hope could he possibly possess if she was gone from his life?

He could see the flashing lights of the police cars in the distance, and knew he really had no choice. It would be up to Gail to embrace him or reject him, but he would leave it to her to decide. Without her, his life held no purpose . . .

He began walking back through the shadows, his torn clothes fluttering in the gentle breeze. He still didn't know what he would say to her, how he would explain what had transpired before her very eyes, but somehow, he hoped she would understand. He still believed that she was ready to help him escape from the purgatory he had been sentenced to. That she was his only hope to avoid the damnation threatening his soul . . .

Kolak walked steadily onward. He could see the empty police cars, the lights still slashing through the darkness, the bodies having been whisked away by the wailing ambulance, the officers searching for those responsible. He was in the midst of crossing the street when his eyes fell upon her.

"Gail!"

She turned with tears in her eyes, and hurried toward him. They fell into each other's arms, their lips meeting in tender caress, the long evening melting away in passionate fervor.

"I knew you'd come back," she whispered.

"I had to," he replied. "It just seemed so pointless without you."

She smiled, grabbed his hand, and led him to the other side of the street. They stood there staring into each other's eyes.

"Then it's true," she said. "The tiger spirit inhabits your soul—"

"But I've learned how to control it, and now I think I know how to rid myself of it forever."

"We can finally be free—"

"Yes, my darling, free to do all those things we dreamed about—"

He paused as a high-pitched shrieking pierced the air. There were groans and shouts, and then he turned, and began dashing into the darkness. She watched as he vanished among the shadows, hurrying after him, wanting to protect him from what she feared he would find. As she reached the old Victorian house, she could hear the snarling emanating from the tangled darkness, and slowed her pace.

"He was trying to destroy all that is ours," hissed one of the figures standing there in the misty gloom. "And so, I shall destroy him instead."

It was Lil in the form of the hyena creature she had revealed to them inside the house. She was holding Detective Dempster in her arms, Detective Coggs lying on the ground groaning. Kolak stood nearby, attempting to convince her not to harm them until they were given a chance to explain their actions.

"Somebody throw the gasoline on her," Dempster gasped. "It's the only way!"

"So now you understand, Mr. Kolak," sneered the creature. "That's the explanation you seek."

She snarled once again, and then Gail dashed forward, grabbed the gasoline can and threw the liquid at her. The creature screeched her displeasure, bit into Dempster's neck, and hurled him to the ground.

Dempster grabbed his neck, tried to stop the flow of blood, and then twisting in pain, reached into his pocket and pulled out a silver lighter. As the creature staggered forward, Dempster ignited the flame, leaned over, and collapsed on the creature's leg.

The creature howled in anger, and then suddenly, the flames burst upon her leg and raced toward her head. In a matter of moments, the creature and Detective Dempster were engulfed in the raging fire.

They could hear the creature howling in pain as the flames sizzled and hissed, totally consuming her body. Gail screamed, then directed

Kolak to pull Dempster's burning body away from the yelping creature. He responded, and soon the detective was smoldering in the damp soil. There was still blood oozing from the neck wound, and as they rolled him over, they could see his eyes were opened wide and his mouth frozen in lingering agony.

Then they watched as the burning creature staggered forward, and what appeared to be some sort of malevolent apparition emerged above her flaming head. The apparition let out a terrifying scream and then suddenly vanished amid the cool, misty air. The creature stumbled toward the old Victorian house, finally falling against the brown-shingled wall, and crumpled into a pile of glowing ash and embers. The flames, meanwhile, continued to burn, shooting up the wall of the old house, crackling and snarling against the pale gray sky. Apparently, the detectives had soaked the wall in gasoline before being spotted by Lil.

"We'd better get away from here!" shouted Kolak. "This whole house is going to go up in flames!"

As he turned around, a blanched face appeared in the pale moonlight, scratched and bloodied. It was Charlie Endor, and as he stepped forward, Gail let out a piercing scream.

"Charlie, it's no good," said Kolak, stepping backwards. "Lil is dead. It's over and nothing can be done about it."

Endor's mouth opened, sending a lugubrious moan drifting through the darkness. Then the towering figure stepped forward, and with an echoing howl, leapt into the hissing flames. Kolak watched as his body crashed through the scorched wall, became ensnared in the roaring fire, and then suddenly shriveled into a mass of flaming cinders. A snarling howl resounded through the burning house, and then faded amid the flash of glistening sparks that shot up toward the burning ceiling.

Kolak turned away and glanced at Gail. She looked as if she were about to scream again, so he opened his arms and let her fall against him. He held her for a few moments, and then turned back toward the blaze.

"Let's get him away from here," he finally said, pointing at the fallen Detective Coggs.

He reached down, heard the detective groan in response, and then, letting go of Gail, carried him toward the street. Gail had the detective's other arm wrapped around her shoulders as they shuffled toward the flashing lights of the police cars.

They stood there in the early morning darkness watching the flames steadily devour the old house. After a while, the voices of spirits echoed through the air, their ghostly images glowing in puffs of light above the burning structure. There were hideous faces and the sound of wicked laughter, many of the images in the process of performing some damnable or depraved act. And then when the images sizzled and faded into the darkness, other images appeared to roil the misty air in shrieks of contempt and malevolence. The unabated rancor continued until finally the last of the images flickered like candlelight and melted into the pale gray sky. The flames, meanwhile, leapt out the windows and licked at the walls, engulfing the entire structure in the blaze.

"And now you are finally free, Roger," whispered Gail with a taut smile. "No longer are you the captive of the spirits."

He looked at her and nodded. "Now we can live our lives as we had planned," he said. "My other soul has been liberated."

He put his arms around her, and they watched the flames stirring in the morning breeze. The twinkling of light was spilling across the darkness, and soon, great clouds of black smoke could be seen billowing in the air. They could hear the shouts of police officers behind them, returning to their cars in a mad rush of apprehension.

"Well, what do we do now?" asked Kolak, watching as one of the officers dashed toward him. "They're going to want to know who we are."

"You let me worry about that," said Detective Coggs, lying on the pavement. "After all, you helped save my life and many others."

The detective reached into his pocket and removed a set of keys. "Here, you take it, Kolak," he said. "I'll be in the hospital for a while, anyway. There's a clean suit in the trunk. Bring the car back to the precinct and we'll forget the whole thing and call it even. I'm giving you a second chance because your girlfriend helped us out and she believes you weren't responsible for those murders. I'm going to agree, but if you're involved in anyone getting hurt again, I'll throw the book at you. Understand?"

Kolak grabbed the keys and looked at Gail. "It's our ticket to freedom," he said with a grin. "We can begin again."

Gail smiled, wrapped herself around his arm, and kissed him on the cheek. After several minutes, the ambulance arrived and the detectives were taken away. Kolak and Gail got inside the black sedan and noticed Jessie was still sitting in the back seat.

"Our leaders are dead and the coven has been destroyed," she said, wiping a tear from her eye. "The spirits are not pleased."

"But now you're free to go wherever you like," Gail replied. "Don't you see? It's best for all of us."

"We will never be free," said Jessie. "We are minions of the spirits."

"But you do have somewhere else to go, don't you?" asked Gail. "I mean, you must have family—"

"The coven is my family. And what about you, Mr. Kolak? Do you think you're free to go where you like?"

Kolak nodded. "It's over, Jessie," he said. "Charlie and Lil are dead, their souls destroyed forever—"

"But you still live, Mr. Kolak," she said. "And you also possess the power of the spirits."

"I'm afraid you're wrong. The tiger spirit has left my body forever. I no longer possess the power of the turnskin. I think you're going to have to look elsewhere for a leader. I'm just an ordinary man. I want nothing more than to continue the life I once knew. Can't you understand that?"

"Are you quite sure, Mr. Kolak?" she replied. "It seems your desire is actually quite different than what is. Do you really think you can lead a normal life after all that has occurred? Do you think you can be happy knowing you possess the power of the other soul?"

"I told you, the tiger spirit is gone. I have no use for it anymore. It was all just primitive superstition, anyway. Don't you understand? Gail and I are going to settle down and be very happy together and there's nothing that will ever get in the way of our love again."

"Then I guess that is what you choose to believe," said Jessie. "But we have all seen the power you are capable of. If you choose to disregard it, then that is your choice."

Kolak glanced at Gail, who wore a look of concern. "It is gone, isn't it, darling?" she asked passionately. "Oh, tell me she's wrong."

Kolak smiled. "It's gone, Gail," he finally said. "It left me along with all those other spirits you saw tonight. I realize now you and the doctors have been right all along. It was all just an hallucination. But I don't believe in hallucinations any longer, only the future of our love."

A contented grin spread across Gail's beautiful face, and then believing the nightmare had finally ended, she leaned over and kissed him. He looked back at Jessie, who was sitting there staring at them with an angry grimace.

"Well, anyway, you're free now, Jessie," he finally said. "Is there any place you would like us to take you?"

Jessie slowly shook her head. "I belong here with the others," she replied. "It is, I believe, where you also belong, Mr. Kolak. But, anyway, we will meet again." She then opened the door, and in a moment, was gone.

"What did she mean by that, Roger?" Gail wondered.

"I don't really know," he said, starting the engine. He paused for a moment to see if any police officers were going to stop them. "Where are we headed?" he finally asked.

"Back to the city," smiled Gail. "There's no longer any reason why we can't. There's no one looking for you any longer, Roger. Why, we can pretend none of this ever happened."

He nodded, stared ahead into the dim morning light, and watched as the fire engines pulled up behind them. He glanced back at the old Victorian house and could see dark plumes of smoke rising into the misty air.

The car rumbled along the highway, the sun glistening in the blue sky above. They were headed back to New York City, back to the life they had left unfinished all those months ago. Kolak thought the realization of that fact would leave him peaceful and grateful, but something was bothering him. Was the tiger spirit really gone, and if not, what would happen to their relationship if it suddenly appeared upon his writhing visage? And if it did once again emerge, was he confident enough to be able to control it and avoid doing any serious harm to Gail? Kolak thought about it and felt a shiver dance through his body. He began to worry that any kind of stress could possibly send him into a sprawling fit. He wondered how Gail would react, and whether he would suddenly be on the run once again . . .

"It's beautiful, darling, isn't it?" he heard Gail say.

"W-What is?" he stammered.

"Why, everything," she gushed. "The day, the sky, our future together—beautiful."

"Yes, beautiful," he mumbled.

"But whatever is the matter, Roger?" she asked. "You look worried about something—"

"It's nothing really," he replied, trying to come up with an adequate explanation. "I was just thinking about everything that has happened. You know, Charlie and Lil and Dr. Chen—"

"Well, I would say it would be best to forget all about them. What happened has happened, and couldn't be avoided. There was nothing anyone could have done about it. Let's just be thankful that we didn't suffer the same fate." She paused. "Anyway, we're supposed to be starting a new life together, darling. Let's not spoil it with talk of tragedy."

"But it's not over yet, Gail," he said. "I mean, we're riding in a detective's car. I'm sure they'll be looking for us before too long. I mean, we're witnesses—"

"The detectives will handle everything," she calmly replied. "I think Detective Dempster will be all right eventually, and Detective Coggs only suffered minor injuries. And they saw everything we saw, Roger."

He looked back at the road and fell silent. He realized Gail was prepared to put the past behind them as soon as possible. How could she not have been severely affected by the whole ordeal? Was she actually selfish and unsympathetic or just attempting to elude a painful experience by focusing on the present?

He stared at the highway and wondered what the police would do to the members of the coven who were captured? Would they eventually begin again in another coven, or would they go back to their families and venture down new and more promising paths? And what about his own situation? Would he ever receive any more grant money for research after everything that occurred?

"Relax, Roger, it'll all work out somehow," she said, almost as if she was reading his mind. "I mean, we could always leave New York and go somewhere else—"

Somewhere else. He liked the sound of that. Somewhere they didn't know his name, somewhere far away from New York, Malaysia, shamans, and curses. He squinted into the glaring sun. As long as she would be there, wherever that would be, with him . . .

"You wouldn't mind leaving New York?" he asked tentatively.

She looked at him. "There's nothing keeping me here," she finally said. "I can always find another job wherever we wind up."

He smiled his approval. "Probably something better than what you have here," he said.

"Yes, maybe," she replied.

He leaned back and thought about where they might go. Florida? California? Arizona? Some place where the weather was warm and the sun sparkled in the sky like a blazing gem, and the water was cool and clear . . . somewhere else. There was no need to remain in New York where the winter wind pierced your skin and the steamy summer air wrung the sweat from your body. *Somewhere else . . .*

As they traveled through the streets of the city, a renewed vigor began to pulse through his body. *Maybe it all will work out.* He glanced at the people scuttling through the streets, the towering buildings slashing through the clouds, and Gail's radiant face. She remained optimistic throughout it all and the feeling began to seep deep down into his bones. This was the city of dreams, and anything was possible . . .

They left the detective's car in front of the police precinct and walked home in the hazy sunshine. Gail was right; no one had stopped them, no one was looking for them. They were free to begin again.

"And now do you believe me?" she asked, her face turned toward the sun. "We're free to do as we like. There's no longer anyone chasing you."

"It will take a few days to forget," he replied. "Then we can think about what to do next."

She looked at him and smiled, and he felt as if a great storm had passed. It was as if he had finally returned from Malaysia. He grabbed her hand, held it tight, and looked up into the deep blue sky. As long as he had Gail, there was no need to fear the future . . .

The days passed. He had moved his things into Gail's apartment and the world seemed to grow a little brighter. He had begun to forget about the curse, the coven, the shaman, as if it was some sort of nightmare that seemed so real at the time, and yet, had vanished with the morning. The only thing on his mind now was Gail. How her name flitted through his brain with sparkling contentment. She was part of his world once again, and her face, her words, her very being, glistened through his soul. Their relationship was once again vibrant and alive, ever growing, with a future that knew no bounds.

And then the night came. She was removing her clothes, readying herself to surrender to him, and then he knew somehow that all the suffering he had gone through was for a reason. It all made sense now. He could now appreciate Gail's warmth and affection more than ever. She still believed in him, was still willing to make love to him, and everything suddenly had a purpose.

"You're so beautiful, Gail," he said, watching her undress. "How I dreamed of this moment. A return to normalcy and the past."

"You know I always loved you, Roger," she replied. "Those days before you left for Malaysia were some of the happiest moments of my life."

He stared at her supple breasts, the nipples erect, and the lithe, curving figure punctuated by her moist tuft of pubic hair. It reminded him of a particularly sunny summer day, golden sunshine and the sweet scent of lilac. Her blonde hair glistened in the dim light.

He felt the pleasant urge seizing his mind and body once again, the stirring of his member, as it stood up and stretched toward his taut stomach. He unfastened his pants, felt the straining and stretching inside, somewhat reminding him of his bodily transformations of the past. There was almost that same thrill, that same ecstasy of change, swelling through his coursing blood, his every flexed muscle. Yes, the sexual arousal, combined with the stretching and straining, made the two sensations very similar. The only difference was the stimulus—the breathtaking vision of blonde beauty standing before him.

He slid his pants down, unsheathing his pulsing member, and removed his shirt. Then he slid over to her beckoning body, and ran his hands along the curvature of her torso. He then found the firm breasts, and her body melted next to his.

"Oh, Roger, could it really be as good as I remember," she said. "If only it could be like it was, before . . ."

"Forget about time, my darling," he replied. "There is only the two of us."

He slid on top of her, groaned, and felt his member sink into her warm embrace. He felt it writhe among the warm, slick surface hidden between her straddled legs, and then he threw his head back and grunted with satisfaction.

He closed his eyes, and could feel the ripples of transformation undulating across his skin. He kept bucking his hips, enthralled with the sweltering wetness of her body, when he felt the hair begin to germinate, sprouting up through the pores of his skin. He grimaced, clenched his teeth, and could feel the straining of his muscles as they swelled and bulged. He felt his member tighten against the walls of her vagina, suddenly swelling inside her. Her moaning reverberated through the room, echoing inside his brain. His hands clung to her breasts, until he felt his fingers begin to grow, and then darken with the propagation of hair. When the nails began to lengthen, he pulled his hands away, and let out a snarling growl. He could now see the graceful body below him tinged with yellow, and he knew he had become the beast once more. He glanced out the window, could see the moon as bright as a silver amulet, and then threw back his head. The orgasm gushed through his body, poured out through his member, and made him shudder. He began to roar, a renewed vigor flowing through his mind and body, and as he closed his eyes, he could feel the harshness of the past slowly fade into the darkness of the night . . .

Kolak opened his eyes. He was sitting on top of Gail, panting with utter contentment, the sweat beading up on his naked human body. He had never felt such an intense feeling before. The hair, the nails, the fangs were gone. He was once again a man, and as he looked down, he could see Gail's head turned to one side, sighing like an autumn breeze.

"Are you all right, Gail?" he asked, hoping he hadn't injured her amid the hallucination.

She turned her head, and looked up at him with a weary smile. "Oh, Roger, I didn't think it could ever be so good," she said. "That was the most intense orgasm I've ever had."

He bowed his head, happy that he had pleased her, but knowing the beast still lingered inside the dark recesses of his brain. But he told himself that he would forget with the passing of time. *Time.* That's all he needed.

"Roger, would you like to get rid of that curse once and for all?"

He looked at her, and nodded his head. "Nothing would please me more," he said.

"Well, Dr. Keld seemed to think there was one more chance. He said a Dr. Emery Glyco might be able to help you. There would be no psychiatry, no mental hospitals. It would be totally scientific. Would you want to give it a try?"

Kolak paused. He thought to himself he really had nothing to lose, and if medical science was involved, maybe there was still a chance they would be able to find a cure. His happiness with Gail depended on it.

"I'll give it a try, Gail," he finally said. "For you."

13

THE SCIENTIFIC METHOD

THEY STOOD THERE IN THE middle of the antiseptic white room, looking at the cages filled with mice and rabbits. Kolak was no longer nervous about surrendering himself to the doctors. This was no longer a case involving a malady of the mind, but was now being treated as an illness of the body that could possibly be cured by modern science.

"Hello, Mr. Kolak, it's nice to meet you," greeted a white-haired doctor wearing a bright white medical gown. "I'm Dr. Emery Glyco. Dr. Keld explained to me the details of your particular case."

"Then you think you can help him, doctor?" asked Gail.

"Yes, of course," smiled Dr. Glyco. "You see, I have studied this particular disease and have found that it's very similar to a rare genetic condition known as progeria."

"What's that?" asked Kolak.

"Progeria, my friend, is a rare disease that causes the premature aging of children, and was first described in England in 1886 by a Dr. Jonathan Hutchinson. Now while it might not be exactly what you suffer from, there is an incidence of a transformation of the body, which is very similar to the characteristics of your case. It's also similar in the fact that progeria is not an inherited condition. The disease causes a transformation of the body, however, in a short period of time, leading to dwarfism, baldness, loss of body fat, and aged-looking skin. It's very similar to another skin disease you may suffer from called porphyria. You see, we have been studying the model of premature aging to provide us with a better understanding of what occurs in the body as we grow older. I think this may have something to do with your current condition. A condition, I might add, that may have been hiding inside you since birth."

"Well, is there a cure?" asked Kolak.

"There might be, Mr. Kolak," said the doctor. "You see, we now believe this particular disease is caused by a single abnormal gene in the region of chromosome one. We were helped by the completion of the map of the human genome, and have found that the gene involved, lamin-A, produces proteins that help the cell's nucleus hold its contents during cell division. Now, the possible cure to this disease we think involves gene therapy."

"Gene therapy?"

"Gene therapy, Mr. Kolak, is an experimental medical method that involves modifying the genetic material of living cells to fight disease. Our goal is to supply cells with healthy copies of missing or altered genes. So instead of giving a patient a drug, we attempt to correct the problem by altering the genetic makeup of some of the patient's cells."

"So there is something wrong with my genes?"

"We think so, Mr. Kolak. You see, genes determine such traits as physical strength, and can be influenced by environmental factors. According to Dr. Keld, you experience changes in these traits when you are affected by the transformation."

"Yes, that's true," Kolak said. "There's a total change in my entire physical form."

"Now to combat that, we'll inject a gene into your body which will help your body fight against your illness. The only problem is we can't inject a gene directly into your cells, so we'll have to use a carrier known as a 'vector.' The most common type of vectors are viruses because they can enter a cell's DNA. But don't worry the toxic DNA of the virus will be removed so it doesn't cause additional illness. The advantage of this treatment is that it doesn't require powerful and dangerous drugs.

Instead, the body uses its own cells to combat the disease, and doesn't need donor cells of any kind."

"Is there any risk involved?"

"Well, Mr. Kolak, like with any new treatment there are, of course, risks. The first genetic treatment was administered in 1990, and then in 1999, a patient died from a reaction to a gene therapy treatment. But I want to assure you that in the years I have been using gene therapy, not one patient has died or even experienced severe illness. The decision, however, is still up to you."

Kolak looked at Gail, and then smiled. "It's my only chance at happiness," he said. "If it works, Gail and I will be able to lead a normal life again. And if it doesn't, my situation will not have changed. So I guess the only thing to do is give it a shot."

"Good, good," Dr. Glyco replied. "Then we can begin the injections right away."

Kolak began the gene therapy injections, optimistic that this was finally the cure he had been searching for. He began to research the method and had found it had temporarily cured mice of diabetes.

"Look at what it says here in this literature," he told Gail. "The gene therapy triggered cells in the liver to produce insulin and other hormones."

"Yes, Roger, Dr. Keld had great hope for the treatment," she replied.

"It says here that doctors in Houston used a gene called NeuroD to get the liver to produce beta cells to make insulin, hormones, glucagons, somostatin and pancreatic polypeptide, all helping regulate insulin production and release."

"Certainly sounds like a cure," smiled Gail.

"Another disease approved for the treatment was ADA deficiency, a rare genetic disease. People born with the disease don't produce a necessary ADA enzyme. And it's caused by a defect in a single gene, which they say increases the likelihood that the therapy will succeed."

"Were they cured?" asked Gail.

"Says here their immune systems improved after they received gene therapy. And now they're producing the ADA enzyme on their own."

"That's wonderful, Roger," she said. "It's truly the cure we've been searching for."

Kolak nodded his head, and then holding her hand, they walked home.

"We can begin to plan our future again, Roger," she said, as they reached the apartment. "As long as you keep taking the injections, we really don't have anything to worry about."

Kolak smiled. "It's as if all of this had been a dream," he said.

"A nightmare is more like it," she replied. "But maybe we're just starting to reawaken, realizing all of it has no bearing on our future."

Gail's optimism echoed in his ears, causing thoughts of a future to reappear in his brain. *Yes, maybe it will all work out, after all.* There was no longer any reason to believe he couldn't begin once again. Maybe even undertake a new study of human behavior. He certainly had accumulated enough experience to complete such a study.

Feeling almost as if his life had been resurrected, Kolak began to look forward once again to what could be. He had potential again, his tattered dreams mended by the miracles of science. And then the night came.

He was reading the newspaper, trying to reacquaint himself with the events occurring in the world, when he happened to glance up at the window. A full moon glowed in the night sky, shimmering in the darkness like the eye of an evil specter. He tried to ignore it, telling himself that the therapy had effectively vanquished his fears, when he suddenly realized he was sweating.

"No, it can't be," he muttered to himself. "The therapy was supposed to prevent this from happening."

He tried to relax, tried not to think about it, and kept on reading the newspaper. He found it hard to concentrate, however, and placing down the newspaper, stood up. He wiped his forehead with his hand, and much to his surprise, it felt dry. The sweating was gone.

He walked over to the window, and began pulling down the shades. He told himself that if he couldn't see the moon, then it couldn't affect him. As he pulled down the last shade, he glanced at his right hand and noticed a clump of coarse hair had appeared. He ran his fingers through the hair, and then felt the sweat return to his body.

"Damn," snarled Kolak. "If Gail sees me like this, everything we had planned will be destroyed. She won't understand. Why aren't the damned injections working?"

Kolak began to get nervous, and sat back down. The only thing to do was try to relax. He looked back at his hand. The coarse hair was still there. He sat back in the easy chair, and closed his eyes. If he could fall asleep for a few minutes, maybe it all would pass.

Kolak tried to drift off to sleep, but it was impossible. All he kept thinking about was why the injections hadn't prevented the beginnings of the transformation. He opened his eyes, and looked down at his right hand. The coarse hair had vanished along with the sweat. Maybe the injections were working, after all. Maybe his body was becoming accustomed to fighting the transformation symptoms. That was probably it, he told himself. There had to be some form of the transformation for his body to know what it was fighting. Kolak began to calm down, and picked up the newspaper. He began reading an article on the mayor's wife when he felt his body begin to contort. Strange sensations were running through his arms and legs, and he felt the urge to jump out of the chair.

He put down the newspaper, and felt the rippling sensations move through his shoulders. Was he changing? Would the injections prevent any further transformation?

He felt as if the muscles were bulging and stretching on his right side only, and he looked down. Yes, the muscle in his right arm was bulging. The left side, however, appeared to remain normal. Kolak clenched his teeth, and grabbed the armrests of the chair. If he were going to change, he would do it sitting down and calm as possible.

"Roger, are you ready to go to dinner?" he heard Gail shouting from the bedroom.

Gail. What if she saw him like this? What if she saw him transform into the beast? What if she realized the gene therapy injections were not working like she had hoped?

Kolak clung to the chair, and waited for the worst to happen. The sensations, however, were suddenly subsiding. The bulging in his muscles were disappearing, slowly returning to normal. The injections were definitely helping, he told himself.

Then the bedroom door opened, and Gail strolled into the room. She looked at him, and smiled. Apparently, he was back to normal.

"I thought we'd eat at that Italian restaurant down the block," she said. "I'm in the mood for some nice veal."

Kolak stood up, tested his arm, and nodded his head. "Fine with me," he said. "I'll have the lasagna."

She walked up to him, and kissed him. "That's the Roger I used to know," she said. "I'm so glad the injections are working. Now, if you're a good boy, you might even get some dessert tonight."

Kolak smiled. "I think I'll eat fast," he said.

They laughed, put on their jackets, and walked out the door holding hands. Kolak hadn't felt so good since he left for Malaysia.

"You know, things are really starting to get a little better," Gail said with a smile. "Before you know it, this whole thing will have passed from our memories."

"I sure hope so," Kolak replied. "Maybe I'll apply for another grant soon."

"Oh, Roger, do you really mean it? That's fantastic. But I really don't want you going so far away this time. I mean, you still may be susceptible to things—"

"You mean like to the local voodoo?"

"You know what I mean, Roger. Your health is still fragile, why go anywhere that may harm it?"

He smiled, not wanting anything to get him upset. "Okay, Gail," he said. "Maybe you're right. Anyway, we'll wait to see what the doctor says after some more injections."

"That's the Roger I once knew," she replied. "Eminently practical."

When they came to the restaurant, he opened the door, and they slipped inside. The waitress showed them to a nice candlelit table near the wall.

As they sat down, Gail smiled at him. "You know I didn't realize you didn't shave today," she said.

The words made Kolak stiffen in his chair. He instinctively put his hand up, and felt his chin. There was a growth of hair under his fingers. But he had shaved this morning. Could it be he was going through the transformation again?

"Must have missed a spot," he said with a laugh.

Then he looked down at his right hand. A small clump of coarse hair had reappeared. He quickly shoved the hand under the table, hoping Gail wouldn't notice.

"Now, remember, the doctor said no alcohol," she was saying.

He nodded his head, and glanced back down at his hand. The hair had spread to the lower part of his arm.

"Maybe we should eat the food at home—"

"Is there something wrong, Roger?" she asked.

"No, I just thought it might be, you know, more romantic."

"You are a tiger, aren't you, Roger?" she said with a smile.

He tried to smile, knowing that what Gail said might be more truthful than she imagined.

"That's funny," she said, staring at his face. "I guess that wasn't hair, after all. Must have been the shadows from the candle."

Kolak raised his left hand to his chin. The hair was gone. He didn't know what to do. Should he tell her that the injections hadn't eliminated his ability to transform?

Kolak stayed silent, and when the waitress came, they ordered their food and waited.

"What's wrong with your hand?" she suddenly asked.

"Oh, nothing, I banged it in the apartment."

"Let me see it."

"It's really no big deal, Gail—"

"Is there something wrong, Roger? I mean, you've been acting strange since we sat down—"

"Nothing, really."

"Let me see your hand, Roger."

He hesitated for a moment, wondering what she was going to say or do, and finally slowly lifted the hand.

"There's not even a scratch," she said. "Your hand, Roger, is perfectly fine."

He looked at it, noticed the coarse hair was gone, and placed it down on the table.

"It felt worse than it looked," he said.

When the food finally came, Kolak was still worried Gail might notice something. He tried to remain calm, and began eating his food.

"You know, the injections were the best thing to ever happen to us," she said. "I only wish Dr. Keld was around to see it."

"He was a good man," Kolak replied. He glanced down at his right hand, and seeing that the hair had not grown back, began to feel confident that everything was returning to normal again. Must be just a few side effects of the injections, he told himself.

"This is absolutely the best veal," she was saying.

He looked up, smiling, when he realized his vision was tinged with a yellowish glow. The transformation was beginning again. He bent his head back down without a reply, and continued to eat, not wanting anything to disturb their dinner together.

"How's yours, Roger?" she asked.

He dared not look at her. "Fine," he finally said, without picking up his head.

"Well, you seem to be enjoying it."

Kolak was relieved when they finally finished, and were ready to head back to the apartment. He still didn't know what he would do if the transformation occurred. Without any food to distract her, however, he had no choice but to pick his head up and look at Gail.

"I think those injections are working just fine," she said, staring into his eyes. "You're looking better than ever."

Kolak sighed, the yellowish glow having faded from his eyes. Maybe there wouldn't be any transformation, after all.

"Feeling just fine," he finally replied.

Gail smiled, threw her arms around his waist, and gave him a coquettish kiss.

"Ready for dessert?" she asked.

Gail looked at him, and smiled. "Well, I don't think the injections affected your sexual prowess," she said. "You were terrific as usual."

Kolak smiled back. He had made love to her again, and although he felt as if the transformation was about to come bursting through his mind and body, it never fully materialized. He was sure the injections had something to do with it. He watched as Gail slid out of bed, and fully naked, sauntered to the bathroom in a rhythmic splendor that captivated his soul. Surely, she was enough of a reason not to want to go through the transformation ever again.

He laid back on the bed, his head engulfed by the softness of the pillow. Yes, Gail. As long as she was with him, he decided anything was possible. In a few months, he would schedule another trip to somewhere, continuing his studies into the origins of human behavior. He had already found the beast within, and now would study how that creature affected the development of human society.

His thoughts of restarting his career were suddenly interrupted by Gail, who was strolling back to the bed. The firmness of her breasts and the contour of her elegant body made him smile. She was truly as beautiful as he remembered during his long stay in Malaysia. She was worth every moment he spent thinking and dreaming about her.

"It's getting late, Roger," she said with a yawn. "I think I'm going to go to sleep. How about you?"

"Yeah, I am pretty tired," he replied. "Are you coming with me to the doctor?"

She nodded her head. "Of course, Roger," she said. "I'm just as interested in your therapy as you are."

He smiled. "Did I tell you how much I love you, Gail? I mean, how important you are to everything I do?"

"Oh, Roger, you're so important to me—"

He leaned over and kissed her. Their lips melted together, and then he moved on top of her, and she suddenly pulled her head away.

"Really, Roger," she said. "We have to get some sleep. We're not teenagers anymore. We can't just keep making love until the morning. The doctor will be waiting for us."

He sat up, and leaned against the pillow. "You're right, of course," he said. "I just couldn't help myself."

Gail smiled. "At least I know you're still attracted to me," she said.

"How could you have thought anything else?"

"There must have been many temptations in Malaysia—"

"Nothing as remotely beautiful as you, Gail."

"That's all I really wanted to know," she said with a smile. "Now let's go to sleep."

Somehow, Gail knew about the others. He turned off the light, and sat in the darkness, thinking that he might have to explain it to her one day. How they didn't mean anything to him, and were just used as part of the process to influence his mind. And then there was Elizabeth. He had made love to her, but she was a werewolf, as much a slave to the transformations as he had been. There was no future for a relationship like that. They had both been deluded, deceived, into believing the transformations were a natural course of their existence, that, somehow, it was a normal part of life to try to control Nature.

Kolak yawned, closed his eyes, and told himself to forget everything that had occurred in the past. He would go to sleep with Gail on his mind, and the thought of her, only her, would guide him through the night . . .

"We cannot die, Kolak."

He stared into Elizabeth's dark eyes, knowing somehow she was right.

"We are guided by the moon and the smell of blood."

Then Elizabeth took his hands, and kissed him.

"No, but Gail," he protested.

"She is not like us, Kolak. She is frail and mortal."

Elizabeth began to laugh.

"No, but you don't understand—"

Elizabeth kept laughing.

"I will die, too, some day."

Elizabeth stopped laughing, and grimaced. "Your soul will live forever, Kolak," she said in a hollow voice.

"No. I will die."

He turned to walk away, and then looked back at Elizabeth. She had turned into a werewolf.

"Come with me, Kolak," she hissed.

"No, I'll stay with Gail. You'll see, we'll be happy together."

Elizabeth howled, and then scampered toward the full moon.

"But you don't know how to control it, Roger."

Kolak turned around, and standing there was Charlie Endor.

"I'm learning, Charlie."

"But we did not have time to show you."

"You taught me enough. I will learn the rest on my own."

"Gail will never understand," he said.

"But she will, she does."

"No, she will never understand—"

"We tried to tell you, Kolak." He looked around for the other voice, and standing next to Charlie Endor was Lil.

"But you said it was a good union, one that could produce Merlin."

"But she does not believe, Kolak."

"She doesn't have to."

He looked at Charlie's face, and noticed that it was a pale white, almost the color of a skeleton. He then looked at Lil's face, and it was also pale white. They stared at him, their eyes wide open and glaring, a querulous grunt echoing through the air. It was the grunt of the beast.

"Come with us, Kolak, we will teach you how to control your other soul," Charlie was saying.

"But you're both dead, and your souls were destroyed by the flames—"

"No, Kolak, our souls still live."

He noticed others behind Charlie and Lil, and tried to peer behind them. He could hear the grunting of the beast getting louder.

"What are you searching for, Kolak?" Charlie asked.

"I'm searching for the beast, the progenitor of man."

"You will never find it, Kolak."

"But I already have, Charlie. In the forests of Malaysia, and within my own soul."

Now he watched as Charlie moved to the side, and behind him, appeared Dr. Chen, his face also a pale white.

"The spirits are not pleased," he said in a droning, hollow voice.

"It doesn't matter any longer," Kolak replied.

"But Erlen Khan has sent me to warn you."

"I'm not afraid," Kolak replied.

"But he commands the Underworld—"

"No, there is another."

Dr. Chen frowned, and as he moved to the side, Dr. Keld appeared.

"Yes, you're right, Kolak, there is another," Dr. Keld said in a low groan. "The true master of the Underworld."

Kolak kept walking, past Charlie and Lil, past Dr. Chen, and past Dr. Keld. There was now only darkness before him. There was a pungent, musty odor in the air, and Kolak knew whatever he was looking for lurked within the shroud of darkness. His sense of smell was more acute than ever. He could feel the beast inside.

"And I stood upon the sand of the sea, and saw a beast rise up out of the sea, having seven heads and ten horns, and upon his horns ten crowns, and upon his heads the name of blasphemy."

Kolak remembered the words that echoed around him. Someone was reading from the Book of Revelation.

"And he had power to give life unto the image of the beast, that the image of the beast should both speak, and cause that as many as would not worship the image of the beast should be killed."

The words swirled through his head, and he kept walking into the darkness.

"And he causeth all, both small and great, rich and poor, free and bond, to receive a mark in their right hand, or in their foreheads . . . Let him that hath understanding count the number of the beast: for it is the number of a man; and his number is six hundred threescore and six."

Kolak looked down at his right hand, and sure enough, there the number 666 was burned into the skin. He felt the beast was close by, and so, he continued walking into the darkness.

"And the beast was taken, and with him the false prophet that wrought miracles before him, with which he deceived them that had received the mark of the beast, and them that worshipped his image."

He looked at his hand once again, 666 branded among the spider-web lines, and continued walking.

"These both were cast alive into a lake of fire burning with brimstone."

Kolak halted when he finally saw the lake of fire in the distance. A great dragon stood nearby shrieking, and Kolak knew at once it was Satan.

"I have come to find the beast," Kolak shouted.

The dragon hissed, and sent a ball of fire hurtling toward him. Kolak moved aside, and the fire went whizzing past him.

"I have come to find the beast," Kolak repeated.

"He is within the soul of man," hissed the dragon in a scratchy tremor. "You, Kolak, bear his mark. Come to me and surrender your soul!"

Kolak trembled for a moment, and then he heard the words of the church service, the organ warbling through the air, the bright light suddenly pouring down from above.

"And I saw an angel come down from heaven, having the key of the bottomless pit and a great chain in his hand."

The words of Revelation floated through the air like a song from the sky. "And he laid hold on the dragon, that old serpent, which is the Devil, and Satan, and bound him a thousand years."

The dragon hissed and spat at the words, sending a tongue of fire toward the light. The fire glistened for a moment, and then went out.

"And cast him into the bottomless pit, and shut him up, and set a seal upon him, that he should deceive the nations no more, till the thousand years should be fulfilled."

Kolak watched as the dragon suddenly vanished. He could hear its wrenching cries below, a huge boulder resting on top of a wide hole in the ground. He then turned, and went back the way he had come, hoping to make his way to the shimmering light above.

"Satan has been vanquished," said Dr. Keld, as he emerged once again from the darkness.

"No, he will be back."

"Did you find the beast, Kolak?"

"He is hidden among the human race," Kolak replied. "I, myself, carry his mark upon my hand."

He then showed Dr. Keld the 666 branded in his right hand.

"You are of the beast, Kolak."

"Yes, I bear the mark."

"We, too, bear the mark, Kolak."

He turned around, and saw Charlie Endor standing there with the number 666 burned into his forehead. He held his right hand up, and there, too, was the number 666.

He then saw Lil, standing next to Charlie Endor, and she, too, carried the mark of the beast on her forehead.

"We are of the beast, Kolak," she cackled.

Kolak turned to his right, and saw all of their victims standing there with eyes wide open and their mouths churning out a song of misery.

"They are of the beast," they chanted.

"We cannot die, Kolak."

He looked at Elizabeth, the number 666 hiding among her long brown hair branded into her forehead.

"But we can and we will," he replied.

"Only the fire of Satan can harm us."

"And our other soul?"

"It grows along with us, Kolak. Guided by the full moon, and the smell of blood in the air."

"No," he said. "Man is guided by superstitions that place him above Nature and a slave to the heavens."

Elizabeth began to howl. He looked at her, and saw that she had changed once again into a werewolf.

"They are of the beast," the others chanted. "They are of the beast."

He then saw the tiger spirit hovering above him, hideously laughing.

"You belong to me, Kolak," he snarled.

"Roger, wake up."

He opened his eyes, and could see that Gail was shaking him out of his dark stupor. It had all been a nightmare.

The first thing he did was to look at his right hand. There was no mark on it, the 666 having faded with the night.

"You were having a nightmare, Roger," Gail said. "By the expression on your face, it must have been horrible."

"I saw Dr. Keld and Dr. Chen."

"Then you were safe."

"Yes, safe," he muttered. "Gail, do we have a Bible?"

She looked at him. "Yes, Roger, it's in the nightstand."

He pulled the drawer open, and removed the black book, quickly turning toward the back. He stopped where it read, THE REVELATION OF ST. JOHN THE DIVINE.

"And before the throne there was a sea of glass like unto crystal," he read. "And in the midst of the throne, and round about the throne, were four beasts full of eyes before and behind."

He kept reading, hoping he could find some sort of answer to the words he heard in his nightmare. "And the first beast was like a lion, and the second beast like a calf, and the third beast had a face as a man, and the fourth beast was like a flying eagle.

"And the four beasts had each of them six wings about him; and they were full of eyes within, and they rest day and night, saying, HOLY, HOLY, HOLY, LORD GOD ALMIGHTY, WHICH WAS, AND IS, AND IS TO COME."

Kolak sat back in the chair, and kept reading. "And when those beasts give glory and honour and thanks to him that sat on the throne, who liveth for ever and ever—"

Then there was hope. Maybe his soul didn't belong to the beast, to Satan. There was another he might belong to.

"Thou art worthy, O Lord, to receive glory and honour and power: for thou hast created all things, and for thy pleasure they are and were created."

Then there still might be a chance, he decided. With the help of the doctors, and a renewed faith, maybe he could live again. And die when his time came to an end. Despite the nightmare, he didn't transform during the night. Maybe there was a greater force protecting him.

"Roger, what are you reading?" Gail asked.

"Revelation, it was part of the nightmare."

"Was God a part of your nightmare?"

"No, but I heard the voices of the faithful, Gail. They were reading from Revelation."

Gail smiled. "Then that's truly a good sign, Roger. There are forces beyond our understanding trying to help you."

"Yes, maybe."

"Oh, Roger, you made me so happy," she said. "With a faith in God, and faith in the injections, maybe we really will be able to start again."

"Yes, maybe," he said, holding the black book in his hands.

14

FAMILIAR FACES

THEY WERE STANDING ONCE AGAIN in the middle of the antiseptic white room, watching the mice and the rabbits look back at them from their cages. Kolak was prepared to tell the doctor about the strange side effects of the injections, and the nightmare he had had during a fitful night. He wondered if the injections were as potent as Dr. Glyco made them seem.

"Here he comes now," Gail said, watching the doorknob turn and the door swing open. "Remember to tell him everything, Roger."

Kolak nodded his head, and watched as the doctor approached.

"Hello, Mr. Kolak," said Dr. Glyco with a smile. "I hope everything is going as planned."

Kolak glanced at Gail, and then shook his head. "Well, there have been some problems," he finally said.

"Oh?"

"Yes, well, I'm afraid the injections haven't totally eliminated my ability to transform," he said. "I mean, I've seen signs, physical signs, that the transformation can occur at any moment."

"But you didn't transform?"

"No, doctor, but there have been unusual growths of hair—"

"Now I never said the injections would have no side effects, Mr. Kolak. We're dealing with an experimental method that is not totally without its problems. But I want to assure you that I have decided to treat you with more than just the injections."

"What else is there, doctor?"

Dr. Glyco smiled. "There are many other things that may be causing your condition, Mr. Kolak. For instance, did you ever ingest any poisons while in Malaysia?"

"There were the plants."

"The plants?"

"Well, the Malaysian shamans used such things as cowbane, hemlock, aconite, poplar leaves, foxglove, nightshade, and cinquefoil."

Dr. Glyco shook his head. "All poisonous plants, Mr. Kolak," he said. "Why didn't you tell Dr. Keld about these plants?"

"I tried to, but there was so much—"

"Now, you see, poisons can disrupt the balance of the enzymes in the cells. For example, diphtheria toxin interrupts the action of a cell's ribosomes, and the toxin in a death-cap mushroom can affect the RNA polymerase and the decoding of DNA. The production of new enzymes is completely halted."

"Is there a cure?"

"Well, I'm going to put you on some antibiotics," the doctor said. "These will help to destroy any bacterial cells in your body."

"Oh, you mean something like penicillin—"

"Yes, Mr. Kolak, penicillin was one of the first antibiotics. It prevents the bacterium from building cell walls. That is important because the cell walls of a bacterium are very different from those of human cells. But all antibiotics work at the enzyme level, and that's very important in dealing with your condition."

"And the injections will continue?"

"Yes, of course, but they might be more effective working in conjunction with antibiotics. That is, of course, if you don't suffer from some virus of some kind. We'll conduct a few tests today. If it is a virus, then we'll have to treat you as soon as possible so that your body can produce the right antibodies against the virus."

"And what about the antibiotics?"

"They will have no effect on a virus," Dr. Glyco explained. "That's why we need to test you as soon as possible. But I still think that you suffer from a genetic problem of some kind, and that's why we'll keep on giving you the injections. It may be that you lack a certain gene for a single enzyme. As I tried to explain to you before, there are many instances of this occurring in the human body—lactose intolerance, for instance, or albinism, or cystic fibrosis. It's quite amazing that if one of your many genes is missing or damaged, it can lead to a problem. Damage to just one enzyme can lead, in many cases, to life-threatening or disfiguring problems."

Kolak listened to the doctor's words, and decided he had complete faith in his ability. Whatever it was that was causing the transformation, he was confident the doctor would find it.

"There's one more thing necessary for the treatment to work," the doctor said.

"What's that?"

"A positive attitude, Mr. Kolak."

"Roger definitely has that, doctor," Gail said. "I mean, since the injections have begun his mental state has been absolutely fantastic. He even has taken to reading the Bible."

"Good, good," the doctor grinned. "Whatever you can do to keep a positive outlook is essential to the treatments working effectively."

The doctor then had Kolak submit to a few new tests, and told him that everything would work out just as he promised.

Kolak and Gail walked home that day feeling relieved.

"It's as if an enormous weight has been lifted from my shoulders," Kolak said. "I feel so confident that the doctor will cure whatever it is I have."

"I am, too," said Gail. "We just have to pray a little bit, and hope for the best."

They smiled at each other, and then headed to a nearby restaurant.

The days passed, and Kolak never once felt as if he was going to transform into the beast. He did have another nightmare, but not as intense as the first one. But as hopeful as he was that the treatments were working, he still felt as if the tiger spirit lingered within his soul. It was a fear he wouldn't dare tell Gail. She wouldn't really understand at this point, he decided. She was so pleased about Kolak's recent mental attitude, he didn't really have the heart to tell her he still harbored some doubts.

Kolak walked along the avenue with a sense of optimism he had not felt for many months. Gail's words of support and encouragement echoed inside him, telling him that whatever the future might hold, she would be there for him, and somehow, it would all work out in the end. He stared up into the bright sunshine, and smiled. Somehow it would all work out. As he came to the corner of the street, he glanced to his left and noticed a woman with long brunette hair standing against a building. She had a familiar look about her, a penetrating gaze he had come to know while staying inside the coven. He looked at her, pausing for a moment to evaluate her face, and then continued walking, deciding it wasn't possible for it to be the same woman.

The coven. The thought of it settled in his mind. Celia Mountainwater, that's whom the woman he had just seen resembled. Celia Mountainwater. But it wasn't possible; she was miles away. He stopped for a moment, suddenly turned, and began hurrying back across the street. He gazed at the building where he had seen the woman, but she was gone. Kolak shook his head, deciding it was only someone who looked like Celia. Without the purple robe, he couldn't be sure.

Kolak waited for a moment, then turned, and crossed the street. Even if it was Celia, maybe she was alone. Maybe the city is where she decided to begin anew. There was no reason to believe any other members of the coven were involved. He kept walking, and then realized someone was looking at him. He turned his head slowly and noticed a man with dark hair and fiery eyes. It was Carl Summerwind, another of the coven members.

Kolak halted and looked back at him. He was just standing there, wearing casual clothing, seemingly waiting for someone or something. Was it Carl, or somebody who just looked like him? He couldn't be sure.

He was about to walk over to him, get a closer look, when some people came strolling down the street from the other direction. He waited for them to pass, and then noticed there was no one behind them any longer. Carl, or whoever it was, had gone.

Kolak searched the surrounding area, but there was no longer any sign of Carl. If it was him, then why would he just disappear like that. Had the coven members decided to get even with him for helping to kill Charlie and Lil? Was this all a part of their plan to seek revenge? He thought for a moment, and then began walking back down the street. He would make his way back to Gail's apartment, think about what to do, and prepare himself for future encounters. If he could only talk to them, explain to them why he had betrayed their leaders, maybe they would begin to understand.

He had gone only a block when he felt as if he were being followed. He looked back and thought he could detect the familiar faces darting into dark alleyways, or into crowds of shuffling people. But they were there, he was sure of it. He began to quicken his pace, looking back every so often, listening for the footsteps pattering along the sidewalk. He reached another corner, turned around, and could see them behind him, gathering together in a group. They were headed toward him, and he tried to think of what he should do. He turned, ready to run, when he stumbled into a small woman with black hair.

"Jessie!" he gasped.

The woman smiled. "I said we would meet again, Mr. Kolak," she said. "You did not believe me?"

"But how, w-why?"

"Because you still possess the spirits, Mr. Kolak."

"B-But I told you, the spirits have gone from me. I'm no longer a captive of the curse."

Jessie smiled once again. "That is what you would have others believe," she said. "But we know better."

Before Kolak could reply, the other members of the coven had reached him, and had surrounded him. He glanced at their faces. Then he was right, it was Celia Mountainwater and Carl Summerwind . . .

"B-But you don't understand," he pleaded. "I no longer possess the powers you speak of."

"You are our leader, Mr. Kolak, there is no doubt of that," insisted Jessie. "You will take your place as the devil of our coven."

"Then there is a coven in the city?"

"Only a temporary one. We will take you there."

Kolak shook his head, attempted to refuse, but the coven members remained adamant. He finally shrugged his shoulders and followed them down the busy avenue.

They had walked for several blocks when Jessie and the other coven members crossed the street and headed for Central Park.

"The coven is on the other side of the park?" asked Kolak, shuffling behind.

"No, Mr. Kolak," replied Jessie. "Our temporary coven is inside the park itself. Wait, and you will see."

"But aren't you afraid the police will find us?" he asked. "I mean, to practice witchcraft in the middle of the city—"

"According to the books I've read, Mr. Kolak, the park is eight-hundred-forty-three acres. Plenty of room to worship and hide."

"But others are bound to see us—"

"Those that are waiting for us will help us escape no matter what the circumstances might be."

"Who are these people?"

"You will see for yourself very shortly," Jessie said. "They are people who know the city better than anyone else, and they have agreed to help us if we allow them to participate in our assembly."

Kolak shook his head and continued following them into the park. They walked for several minutes through the deep blue shadows and the patches of glittering sunlight resting upon the great carpets of green grass when they passed between several trees and emerged into a small verdant field.

Kolak looked around, but couldn't see any sign of anyone else in the area. "But I thought you said there would be people waiting for us," he finally said to Jessie.

Jessie smiled. "They are here, Mr. Kolak," she replied. "We only have to call them for them to appear."

As Jessie turned and began to shout, Kolak wondered whether these people were actually spirits of some kind. After a few minutes, however, a human figure appeared from behind one of the trees. It was an old man, soiled and unkempt, his clothing torn and faded, his hair a tangled mess of dirt and grease. Then several others appeared, men and women also smeared with the filth of the city, their clothing ragged and their faces haggard and rumpled. They slowly stepped out of the shadows, and shuffled across the field, finally halting in front of Kolak and the others.

"This is Mr. Kolak," announced Jessie. "He is our leader and possesses great powers and is able to command the spirits."

Kolak looked at them as they moved closer to examine his bearing. Then one of the old men stepped forward, gazing into Kolak's eyes.

"We are the city people," he said. "We were told you are of the turnskin and can perform great magic—"

Kolak frowned. These were the homeless and hungry of a great city, the impoverished denizens of the darker recesses of the urban jungle, who were expecting magic to feed their bellies and elevate their lives. He stared into their weary faces and decided he couldn't tell them the spirit inside him had vanished, that he didn't possess the powers they expected.

'Good people," he finally said. "Our powers lie within the realm of Nature, and are based upon the wisdom of the centuries. We do not stoop to cheap parlor tricks, but embrace the all-encompassing ways of the natural forces all around us. Our gods are the ancient gods who held dominion over the wind and held their heads in humility toward the Sun. You, too, may embrace the ways of Nature and understand the knowledge of the ages."

When he had finished, he looked at them, hoping they would welcome his words and feel somewhat more optimistic about the future. Their faces, however, didn't reveal joy, but utter disappointment. He glanced at the old man and noticed he was frowning.

"What's the matter?" he asked. "You were expecting us to do magic tricks?"

The old man winced. "But we heard you could perform witchcraft," he mumbled.

"The greatest kind of witchcraft," replied Kolak. "Witchcraft that encompasses the heavens and earth, and the equality of all human beings, regardless of their gender, color, or beliefs—"

The old man looked at him and continued frowning. "But I wanted . . . I thought . . . well, that you could turn all of us into cats," he murmured.

"Cats?"

"Well, you see I've heard those that can perform witchcraft can transform themselves into various animals. And, well, being out on the streets, anyway, I thought maybe you could turn us into cats, something like yourself, and allow us to enjoy the lives we live. I mean, as cats, we would be free of the responsibilities that go along with being people, and yet, we would still be able to maintain our life style as it is—"

"You're talking about familiars—"

"Those that knew us would no longer have to worry about our well-being—"

"Familiars are animal accomplices."

"We would go anywhere you wanted us to go," the old man promised.

Kolak paused for a moment and looked at him. "We don't perform that kind of magic any longer," he said.

"But Mr. Kolak is being modest," interrupted Jessie. "He is one of the chosen who is able to complete the transformation into the beast. I have seen him do it myself."

Kolak grimaced. "But that spirit is no longer contained within my soul," he argued. "I am no longer capable of that feat—"

"—And he can show all of you how to develop your other soul," Jessie continued. "And how to control it to your advantage."

Kolak looked at her, and then glanced back at the others surrounding him. He didn't want to disappoint those that had known so much hardship, but knowing the spirit had gone, he decided they might be satisfied with prayer.

"We are all equal before the gods," he said. "They are the ancient gods, the gods that existed at the dawn of time."

"But we have no need of your gods," said the old man. "We have prayed to our own gods and have never received anything in return. The gods can do nothing for us—"

"They will renew your hope," replied Kolak. "One must have hope in order to perform magic."

"All we ask is that you teach us this magic and help us improve our lives," argued the old man. "Your gods will not give us hope. It's the magic that will do that."

The others nodded at the statement, and then began to grumble their dissatisfaction. Kolak knew he had to do something, so he put his hands in the air, and requested silence.

"Good people," he said. "I will tell you of the other soul, attempt to explain to you how it occurred, and maybe you will understand how difficult it is to control."

They stared at him intently, listening to his words and knowing this was the reason they had agreed to follow the coven members.

"You must be one with the beast," Kolak continued. "You must believe in his spirit and allow it to enter your body, the other soul. You must feel his actions as he prowls through the shadows of the jungle, allow your muscles to move along with his as he hunts down his prey. Only then will you realize the existence of your other soul."

He glanced at their attentive faces, attempting to explain to them what had occurred in the Malaysian jungle, and then he halted for a moment, feeling the sweat begin to build across his forehead.

He could hear the shaman chanting, the beat of his drum pulsing through his mind. He remembered the salve being applied to his skin, the taste of the plant extract, and the murmuring of the Malays as they appealed to the spirits. He saw the tiger once again striding through the forest, the sound of his snarl rising up through the thick, dank air . . .

Kolak staggered forward, could feel the trance engulfing his mind, and fell to the ground. Those around him watched with interest as he began writhing and twitching in the green grass, seemingly unable to control the actions of his thrashing body. The ragged inhabitants of the city had come to see whether the magic they had heard about was real, and now they watched, hoping to witness the actuality of those astonishing stories.

"Is he going through the changes?" asked the old man, edging forward.

Jessie nodded her head. "Yes, he is in the midst of the transformation," she said. "The tiger spirit is taking control of his body, and will soon emerge."

They murmured their agreement in gasps of affirmation, and huddled closer to the twisting body. Kolak looked up, could see them surround him, and wanted to tell them to move away, to run while they still had a chance, but only began gagging in the attempt. He could feel the spirit of the tiger enveloping him, taking possession of his soul.

Meanwhile, the ragged observers stood there, waiting for the magical transformation they had heard about to take place. Jessie and the other coven members attempted to push them back, but they remained adamant in their refusal to move.

The tiger was dashing through the deep shadows, finally spotting his intended victim. His snarl echoed through the air, and then he leaped through the grasping undergrowth, and into the glare of the bright sunshine . . .

Kolak glanced up at the staring crowd, could see them tinged in yellow, and knew the transformation had begun. The intense waves of energy began to pulse through his body, and his muscles began to twitch and bulge. He could hear his clothes tearing under the great strain, and then the other soul began to sprout across his face and limbs . . .

"My God, it's true!" shouted the old man as he stepped back in horror. The others were already beginning to flee, dashing away toward the nearby trees. Jessie and the other coven members also ran, leaving the old man standing there in shock, staring at the growling beast lying on the ground before him.

The beast slowly got up and caught sight of the terrified old man, whose eyes were now wide open in quizzical surprise.

"You fool!" sneered the beast, taking a step forward. He reached out and caught the old man around the neck with his striped hand and snarled. The old man began to gag, his body enveloped in a violent convulsion.

"B-But I thought it was impossible," the old man wailed, his feet now dangling in the air.

The tiger snarled once again, moving his head toward the old man's face, almost touching his nose. He sneered, and then let the old man fall to the ground in a motionless heap.

The beast stood there for a moment, apparently deciding whether to mangle the body, and then snarled his disdain. He could see the others still running away in the distance, sneered, then turned, and headed in the other direction. He staggered toward a clump of trees, his hands held tightly against his head, attempting to take control of his monstrous body, and then fell silently into the soft grass. In the distance, a scream echoed through the calm, warm air.

15

ESCAPE

"THIS IS SHELLEY HARTSWORTH IN Central Park . . . I am standing near the spot where a homeless man has been murdered, his neck broken by a particularly powerful assailant who some say is the deranged human being who police initially thought was an escaped animal, identified by some as a rogue tiger. Police won't reveal the identity of the man, although one police source told me they believe it is the same man responsible for several recent grisly murders, also initially thought to be the work of a tiger. That man, identified as Roger Kolak, was placed in a state hospital, from which he recently escaped. Police caution the public that this man is extremely dangerous . . .

"I have with me a homeless person who claims she witnessed the attack in the park this afternoon. She refuses to give her name for fear the killer may still be after her . . .

"Why were you in the park this afternoon, ma'am?"

"We were told there would be a display of witchcraft by someone who could perform great magic—"

"And that man was Roger Kolak?"

"I believe that's what they said his name was."

"And he was supposed to perform this witchcraft?"

"Well, you see, they said he could transform into the beast."

"And did he?"

"Why, yes . . . I mean, it was the most terrifying thing I've ever seen in my life . . . right there, in front of us . . . why, he became a tiger."

"And you saw him murder that man lying in the park?"

"Yes, it was the beast that did it."

"Thank you, ma'am.

"Now police are saying Kolak's alleged transformation could have been something like an illusion, an elaborate magic trick that may have gone awry. One thing is certain, however, there is a man dead as a result of the demonstration, and that is no illusion. Live in Central Park, Shelley Hartsworth reporting . . ."

Darkness began to settle in the air as the faint rays of the sun drifted to the west, toward a distant horizon. Police officers stood near where the dead body had been found, spattered drops of blood marking the spot. Members of the media stood staring at the spot, their cameras flashing and glaring, illuminating the surrounding landscape.

"We are confident the transformation some of the people say they saw was actually a very convincing hoax," one of the detectives was saying. "Now if the killer is adept at magic, it would explain why he has been able to elude us in the past."

"Then there is no tiger?" asked one of the reporters.

"There is only a man, a human being, responsible for this murder," replied the detective. "And we will find him, no matter what tricks he's capable of."

As the reporters shouted additional questions, the detective grumbled, turned, and began walking away from the blinding lights. He had gone only a few feet when another detective stepped in front of him with a grimace across his face.

"Coggs, what are you doing here?" asked the detective.

"This is my case," he replied. "Mine and Dempster's."

"Well, you were supposed to bring him in. Now weren't you? Apparently, headquarters didn't think you did a very good job."

"But you don't understand, Carrick. Those transformations are not illusions—"

The detective frowned. "I think you'd better go home, Coggs," he said. "You and Dempster need a lot of rest."

"But we actually saw them transform into those beasts," argued Coggs. "Didn't they fill you in on that disease they suffer from?"

The detective's lips curled into a sarcastic smile. "Don't worry, Coggs, we'll take it from here," he finally said. "I understand you and Dempster were under a lot of pressure to bring that maniac in. Well, we'll just have to finish the job for you."

He then frowned once again, and stepping past Detective Coggs, hurried into the shadows of the coming night.

Kolak hurried through the streets, the darkness rippling across the sky. His clothes were torn, his mind still pondering the events of the afternoon. The tiger spirit still lurked within his soul, and something inside him told him it would remain with him forever. How could it be? He had been so hopeful, so optimistic, that there was a chance he could rid himself of it. That even if it did emerge, he could control it somehow. But it had emerged, and now he had killed once again . . .

He thought about Charlie Endor and Lil and how they had attempted to convince him that it was possible to control the other soul and use it to one's advantage. But they had failed to reveal the necessary details, and now both of them were dead. He couldn't control it, he told himself, not to the extent which they had promised. Gail had been right that it could take over his soul, hold him prisoner, and prevent him from doing anything about it.

Gail. The thought of her reemerged in his brain, and as he scuttled through the streets and alleyways, he resolved he would head back to the apartment and attempt to convince her to run away with him. Where they would go was not important. *Somewhere else, anywhere else.* But it was time now to leave, time to go somewhere else and begin again. He only hoped it was still possible.

The thought of the old man glimmered in his mind. Why had he killed him, he wondered. He had wanted to see a display of magic, doubted his powers, arrogantly stood there and watched as he transformed. Yes, that was it, he refused to believe any of it was true until the end. Now he was dead, but not before the realization of the truth . . .

None of them believed it was true, and they had paid for their arrogance. But Gail believed. She had seen him transform into the beast, had watched as he defended her against Charlie Endor. Yes, she believed and now she was the only one who could help him escape . . .

He darted from the alleyway, and crossed the darkened street, heading back toward Gail's apartment. A woman coming from the other direction watched him as he rushed along the sidewalk barefoot, his ragged clothing flapping in the warm breeze. She let out a scream and he headed into a nearby alleyway.

"Carrick, let's put aside our differences," said Detective Coggs from behind. "You see, I know where he's headed."

The detective turned with a frown, and stared into his colleague's eyes. "And where would that be, Coggs?" he asked.

"Back to his girlfriend's place," Coggs replied. "You see, they were going to be married before all of this began. She was helping us to track him down. She thought he could be cured or something."

"And where is this place?"

"Just a few blocks from here. Dempster and I were there only a few days ago. We interviewed her before taking her along with us."

The detective's face seemed to brighten upon hearing the words. He suddenly smiled, put his arm around Coggs, and began walking back toward the cars.

"Sorry what I said, John," the detective apologized. "But you know we're all under a lot of stress to capture this guy. He's making the department look bad. Real bad."

Coggs nodded his head as they reached the police cars. "Of course, I know this is your case," the detective was saying. "Why don't you join us? It'll make everyone look good when we finally arrest him."

Coggs smiled and got inside one of the unmarked cars. Carrick slid into the driver's seat, and the car screeched down the avenue.

Kolak gasped for breath as he made his way up the stairs and down the dim hallway. He halted in front of one of the doors, slid a key in the lock, and opened it. Then he darted inside, closing the door behind him.

"Roger, is that you?" a voice called from inside.

"Yes, darling," he replied. He moved across the apartment, glancing through the window, and drew the shades.

"Is there anything wrong, Roger?" Gail asked, emerging from the bedroom.

She looked at him, could see his torn clothes, and could detect the fear spilling from his eyes. "What on earth is the matter?" she questioned once again.

"We have to leave," he replied with a quick glance.

"Leave? But why?"

"They're after me again, Gail. It's no good, we've got to begin again . . . somewhere else—"

"But Roger, we've only just returned."

"But you said yourself that you'd be willing to leave New York and start again—"

"I know, but you've only tried for such a short amount of time—"

Kolak suddenly motioned to her to be quiet, and listened for footsteps in the hallway.

"Who's after you, Roger?" she finally whispered.

"The police," he replied.

"It didn't happen again, did it, Roger?"

He slowly nodded his head. "I was walking home," he sputtered. "They must have followed us . . . I mean, how else could they know where I was, where I would be . . ."

"Who followed us, Roger?"

"The members of the coven . . . They said I was now their leader and wanted me to go to the park with them . . . They wanted me to explain the other soul to some homeless people and, well . . . it happened again."

"Is anyone dead?"

"I tried to warn the old man, but he wouldn't listen . . . He thought it was all just some magic trick . . . And then I saw him standing there and I couldn't control myself, my other soul . . ."

Gail began to cry, and flinging her arms out, hurried toward him. "I'm so sorry, Roger," she sobbed. "I thought there was a chance, I truly did. And so did Dr. Keld and Dr. Glyco . . ."

"Then you'll leave with me . . . Help me get started far away from here?"

She looked at him her eyes blurred with tears, and slowly shook her head. "No, Roger, I won't be coming with you," she finally said. "I've done everything I can to help you. But don't you see? You tried to seek the necessary help and now you've killed again. I'm afraid there's nothing anyone can do for you any longer. You must give up and allow the police to handle this now. There's no other way."

"But they don't understand the curse, the disease . . ."

"They will in time, my darling. Let them help you before it's too late . . ."

Kolak listened to her words, her voice, and then a strange anger bubbled up from inside him, overwhelmed his mind, and gushed through his eyes, his mouth. "Well, if I'm going to be damned, I'm taking you with me, my darling," he shouted. "We've been through too much together to end it now!"

"No, Roger, please!" she pleaded.

He began to laugh, a hideous cackle that burst forth from deep inside, wrapped his arms around her and began pushing her toward the window. "So you thought this would be so easy, didn't you, Gail, my darling," he hissed with scorn. "That you could leave me whenever you liked—"

"No, please, Roger, you don't understand—"

"I never did understand, did I, my dear? You've always been looking for an excuse to leave me."

She shouted and pleaded, denying his words, and then he threw her against the wall, and opened the window.

"We'll go down the fire escape," he sneered. "Just you and me, and then we'll find a place to hide from them—"

"But, Roger, they'll find us," she cried. "You know they'll find us."

"Maybe not," he replied. "Besides, what chance do I have now? I'm resigned to my damnation, but you, my dear, will not get away so easily."

"But why do this to me? I've only shown you love—"

"Now you don't want to get me upset, my darling. There's still that matter of my other soul. It can emerge at any time. I realize that now. And once it does emerge, there's not that much I can do to control it. Now, do you understand, my darling?"

He pushed her out onto the fire escape landing, and then climbing through the window, ordered her to begin the descent.

As they began climbing down the steps, he reminded her not to scream or shout, and she nodded in reply. Slowly, steadily, they made it to the last landing, and then descended into the alleyway below.

Several minutes later, there was a pounding at their apartment door. The door soon burst open and several police officers and detectives rushed inside. They hurried toward the open window and peered down into the growing darkness. Then, one by one, they climbed through the window and headed toward the alleyway. The brilliant light of the city glowed overhead.

They headed toward the water. Through the alleyways, across the darkened streets, they hurried through the city. Gail tried to scream, tried to cry out to those following them, but the fear and shock of Roger's sudden evil disposition had driven the will to resist from her body. Was this the same man she had given her unequivocal love, her unquestioning concern? She was now afraid to even look at him; his face was contorted with utter depravity, his eyes sparkling with malevolence. She had secretly feared the evil Roger had displayed, his other soul, as he referred to it, would eventually overcome him, but the realization that it had finally occurred caused her considerable anguish. He had changed so dramatically from the days when she was first getting to know him, as if he had been completely engulfed by that other soul. And now she rushed through the streets of the city, his arms wrapped around her, but without the mutual compassion they once shared. It was as if she had been kidnapped by a diabolical reflection of the Roger she once knew.

They shuffled through the gloomy shadows, and emerged from an alleyway, and could see the river, dark and silent, spreading before their eyes. Kolak grunted with perverse satisfaction, and then shoved Gail onward toward the waterfront. He glanced behind him, to see if the others were still following, and then hurried her down the dimly lit street.

"It looks like he's headed toward the river," said one of the police officers, as they made their way down the narrow alleyway. "He's looking for some place to hide."

Detective Carrick halted, and turned toward Coggs. "Let's head back to the car," he said. "We might find him wandering around the docks."

"He can't get very far with a hostage," said Coggs.

"If she's a hostage," Carrick replied. "She's his girlfriend. You said it yourself. She may have gone with him voluntarily. We have no way of knowing at this time."

"But she was doing everything she could to help us find him," argued Coggs. "Somehow I think he knows she betrayed him."

"Now you don't know if that's true. Maybe she wanted to find him so they could run off together." Carrick paused. "Anyway, whatever the truth is, we have a better chance of spotting him from the car."

Coggs nodded, and the two men turned around and headed back down the alleyway. The small group of police officers, meanwhile, hurried in the other direction.

"We'll put out an APB on him and his girlfriend," said Carrick. "If we're lucky, we'll find him by morning."

Coggs grunted his approval as they dashed for the green Chevy sitting in front of the apartment building.

Kolak pushed Gail toward the steps leading up into the abandoned warehouse. She nervously began ascending the steep staircase into the thick darkness, Kolak grunting and shoving her from behind. When they reached the second floor, Kolak retrieved a lighter from his pocket, and flicking it on, held the flame out into the darkness. There was a sudden scamper of tiny feet, most probably of rats, and then all was silent. As they slowly moved inside, they could see the room was filled with multi-gallon metal barrels. Kolak pushed Gail ahead of him, and then inspected the drums.

"Toxic chemicals," he sniggered. "So now we know what the city does with its dangerous liquids—"

"Do you think we ought to stay here, Roger?" asked Gail, trying to stay as calm as possible. "I mean, it may not be safe to breathe in these chemicals."

"Hopefully, the police feel the same way you do, my dear," he replied. "I think this is the perfect place to hide. And there's a window, in case we have to leave in a hurry."

There was silence for a few moments, and then Gail's plaintive voice echoed through the air. "Oh, Roger," she said. "You don't really believe I was trying to harm you in any way? Everything I did was to help you. You must believe that—"

"Then why did you get involved with the police?" he sneered. "Yes, you were trying to help me, my darling . . . Help me back to that hospital and those sadistic doctors—"

"No, Roger, that's just not true. I only wanted to see you cured of that terrible disease. I loved you, Roger, more than you'll ever know. Don't you remember all those things we promised each other?"

"It's no good, Gail," he hissed back. "We're not those two innocent dreamers anymore babbling about a future we knew nothing about. Things have changed, and it's no use trying to disregard all that."

"But you wouldn't harm me, would you, Roger? I mean, things haven't changed that much. There's still all that time we spent together." She tried to look at his face, determine what kind of person he had become, but it was too dark; all she could see was the dim outline of his head and body.

"I don't know, my dear," he finally replied with a hint of a smile. "Maybe Charlie Endor was right all along. I must learn how to control my other soul and use it to my advantage. I must not fear the prospect of killing things it may be the natural course of my existence. Yes, what does it matter if I kill at random these anonymous cretins who serve no purpose on this planet except to struggle with each other over the pointlessness of life? I'm actually doing them a favor. Don't you think so, my darling?"

"But they're human beings, Roger. Have you lost your humanity, as well as any hope for the future?" She paused, and began to sob. "But you studied human beings your whole life. You were an anthropologist looking for the answer to a better world. How can you disregard all that and still call yourself a man?"

"Who are you to judge?" he sneered amid the darkness. "You with your flimsy optimism, hoping everything will work out just as you planned. Thinking you had some control over the events that swirl around you. But you don't, you know. It's all arbitrary and senseless! We have no control over what happens to us, my dear, unless one attains some sort of power, some sort of superiority over ordinary human beings. And that's what my other soul has done for me. It's power, power to control the forces all around us—"

"How, Roger? By indiscriminately killing innocent people."

"Don't you see? I'm invulnerable to the petty annoyances of ordinary life. I can be injured, but not really harmed. And my strength is far superior to that of ordinary human beings. Yes, I have power; the power to cause fear and death."

"But what about all you've studied, all you know about the human condition—"

"I was wrong to want to help them, Gail. I know that now. They're weak, selfish creatures that know respect for only power. That's the way it has always been, my dear. You know that yourself. We came from the beast, and the beast only knows power and survival!"

"No, no, Roger, there are other things. There's compassion and kindness, and empathy for one's fellow beings. These are also qualities which are important to the noble side of the human creature."

"Weakness!" he shouted in reply. "I will have none of it! I will trust my other soul!"

The green Chevy pulled up alongside the abandoned warehouse, a group of police officers standing outside the darkened entrance. Carrick and Coggs emerged from the car and approached the officers.

"He's inside?" asked Carrick, peering into the darkness.

"We think so," replied one of the officers. "We saw him headed in this direction."

"Okay," nodded Carrick. "We can't take any chances. The girl may be a hostage."

"I think we should surround the building," said Coggs. "Call for backup. We want to make sure there's no way he can escape."

"You said he suffers from some disease?" asked Carrick.

"That's what the doctors said," Coggs replied.

"Good, maybe we can use that to lure him out of the building. We can tell him we have doctors coming who think they can cure him. Anything to make him surrender and avoid bloodshed."

Coggs nodded his approval, and watched as Carrick hurried to the car. Then he paused for a moment, knew it was he who had allowed the fiend to escape after the fire at the old Victorian house, and grimaced.

"But, Roger, what do you plan to do?" asked Gail, trying as much as possible to hide the fear that gripped her soul.

"Well, first, I have to destroy those that are pursuing me," he replied with scorn. "Then I must decide what to do about you, my dear—"

"But I pose no threat to you. I've only tried to help you—"

"That was your mistake. Now, I fear, you know too much, my darling. If I'm ever to escape and live like a free man again, I must dispose of those who know anything about me and my curse."

"I have no desire to share that with anyone, Roger—"

"And what's to prevent you from going back to the police or those hideous doctors?"

"You have my word—"

Kolak hissed in reply, and then, a voice crackled through the night air.

"This is the police! We have the building surrounded! Surrender immediately!"

Gail could hear Kolak grunting his disdain, and then he suddenly fell silent. She squinted into the darkness, trying to see what he was doing and whether it was safe for her to run, when a guttural growl echoed through the room.

"Roger?"

A vicious snarl answered in reply.

"Roger, are you all right?"

She paused for a moment, and then noticed the flashing yellow eyes floating through the darkness.

"Don't move, my dear, or I'll be forced to slash your throat," a hissing, sneering voice suddenly said.

Gail shuddered, realizing Kolak had become the beast once again, and then all the fear and the sadness rushed through her mind, overpowering her, and she finally fainted.

"Kolak! We have doctors here who can cure you! Give up while you still can!"

The detective's words fluttered through his mind. He turned away from the direction of Gail's voice, and approached one of the metal drums. Lifting it high over his head, he shuffled across the room and into the darkness.

16

THE DEMONIC SOUL

THE TWIRLING LIGHTS OF THE police cars slashed through the night as officers gathered in front of the abandoned warehouse. Detective Carrick, still holding the megaphone, directed them to positions around the building. He still didn't know whether Kolak possessed a gun or not, and therefore, was taking the utmost precautions to prevent any senseless deaths. There had been no sounds inside the warehouse for quite a while and this concerned Carrick. He had hoped Kolak would have, at least, voiced his disapproval rather than make no reply whatsoever. Their main objective remained getting Gail out of the building alive.

"Kolak! There's no hope of escape! Talk to us while there's still time!"

Carrick looked up into the sky, hoping daylight would arrive sooner than scheduled on this one day of the year. As long as it was dark, escape remained possible.

He looked at Coggs, and they both knew they would soon have to decide what to do next. It was then they heard the snarling rumble through the darkness.

"He's on the roof," said Carrick, rushing behind one of the police cars. "Hold your fire!"

Carrick pointed the megaphone toward the roof and began shouting. "Kolak! Surrender immediately or we will commence firing!"

There was silence for a moment, and then a faint growl echoed in reply. Carrick looked at the other officers and nodded, and shots were fired. A vicious snarl resounded up above, and then a huge object came whistling through the air. It came crashing down upon one of the police cars, a dark liquid splattering in the process, and bounded onto the police officers huddled below. There were soon cries of anguish from the officers bathed in the strange liquid.

"What the hell was that?" shouted Carrick, hurrying toward the fallen officers.

"Some kind of chemical barrel," replied one of the officers kneeling beside one of the groaning men. "The chemical is burning right through their skin."

Carrick shook his head, muttering something under his breath, and then turned toward Coggs, who was standing behind him. "Well, at least, we know he doesn't have a gun," he said. "Someone has to go inside there and find out if we can end this thing."

"If you don't mind, detective, I'd like to volunteer," replied Coggs. "After all, it was my carelessness that led to this whole situation."

Carrick nodded his head. "Good luck, John," he said. "Make sure nothing happens to the girl."

Coggs smiled and headed for the warehouse entrance. He noticed two police officers, their guns drawn, hurrying behind.

"What are they doing?" Coggs asked, turning his head back to Carrick.

"You need backup, John. I'm not sending you on a suicide mission."

The reply seemed to satisfy Coggs. He turned and continued walking. When he reached the darkened entrance, he pulled out his revolver and a flashlight and slowly approached the staircase. The two police officers followed.

"Now you stay behind me," said Coggs. "I don't want anyone else paying for my mistake."

He then began to slowly climb the staircase. After several steps, he halted. He could hear the sound of snarling on the second floor. Pointing the flashlight downward, he hurried up the remaining steps.

The sound of growling and snarling grew louder. He could also hear the sound of metal barrels scraping against the floor.

When he reached the second floor landing, he paused for a moment, listened to the loud grumbling inside, and then rushed inside ready to fire. He threw the flashlight beam toward the fierce snarl, and . . . the hideous face of a roaring beast jumped into view.

Coggs staggered for a moment. He could see the beast standing there, his sharp fangs bared, a metal barrel held high above his head. And then, without thinking any further, he fired a shot.

The beast let loose with a screeching howl, and then the metal barrel came crashing down at Coggs' feet, almost knocking him down the stairs. He leaped inside the room as one of the police officers stumbled behind him. Then he fired another shot. And then another exploded through the room. And then another . . .

A woman screamed, and then the beast staggered into a row of metal barrels and collapsed to the floor . . .

A glimmer of daylight spread across the ominous sky, spilling through a bank of dark clouds, and through the window of the second floor room. Coggs and the other officers edged forward as the light slowly fell upon the beastly form lying there before them. And then, as if by some miracle, the fangs began to shrink, and the snout began to melt back into a man's nose. They stood there, staring in disbelief, as the hair fell from the beast's forehead, and the face began to soften, and slowly, the body began to narrow, compress, and fade back into a human being. The only thing that didn't change was the blood oozing across the man's chest and trickling to the floor.

"Oh, Roger," Gail murmured, watching the transformation. She then bowed her head and began to sob.

"So then the doctors were right," mumbled Coggs to the other officers. "It was some kind of disease."

The officers, still stunned by what they had seen, were about to nod their agreement when the fallen man suddenly opened his eyes and began to cough.

"He's still alive!" gasped one of the officers.

Gail stopped crying, amazed at Kolak's movements, and then knelt down beside him.

"It's no good," he murmured. "You were right."

"Oh, Roger," she moaned. "I tried to tell you—"

"But why, Gail?"

"Because I once loved you, Roger, and I thought your soul was worth trying to save."

"But don't you see? I was never really able to control it. How I hoped that it would leave me and allow me to return to the man I was before. But it was no good. I knew sooner or later it would reemerge, until I had become a prisoner. But you, you Gail, was all that I had left of the man I had been. I was so afraid of losing you. I'm sorry, my darling."

Upon hearing the words, Gail began crying once again. "You warned me from the beginning, Roger, it isn't your fault," she said. "I, too, feared losing all we once had."

There was a renewed glint in Kolak's eyes, as if the man he once was had somehow surged back to the surface. He tried to smile, but it was soon lost amid a sudden gasp for breath.

"Don't move, Kolak," said Detective Coggs. "We have an ambulance coming. You once saved my life, now it's my chance to return the favor. It may not be too late—"

"But it is, detective," replied Kolak. "You see, as long as I live, so does the demon inside me. I can no longer take the chance that it won't reemerge." He then reached down and pulled a lighter from his pocket.

The detective, spotting the spilled chemicals on the floor, threw his hands up and frowned. "I can't let you do that, Kolak," he sputtered.

"But you have no choice, detective," Kolak calmly replied. "You see, it's the only way to destroy the demonic soul." He then turned toward Gail. "You're free now, my darling," he said. "I hope you find some happiness after all this."

She stood up, and one of the officers grabbed her, hurrying her toward the stairs.

"Don't do it, Kolak," Coggs implored.

"I'm afraid I have no choice," Kolak replied. He then flicked his finger and a flame jumped up.

Coggs turned and fled for the stairs as flames erupted through the room. He could hear the crackling and hissing of the fire, as well as a shuddering shriek echo through the building. Then he could hear the sound of voices, like the cries of the damned, reverberate from above. As he dashed outside the warehouse, there was a sudden explosion and the entire building was soon engulfed in flames . . .

It was several moments later that the fire engines came screeching down the street. The leaping flames glowed in the early morning light. Coggs now stood next to Gail and watched the fire consume the building.

"There was no other way, I guess," he finally said.

Gail bowed her head, a glistening tear trickling down her cheek. Kolak's long struggle was finally over.

As the growing light of the new day spilled across the landscape, they stood staring at the charred beams and the smoldering ash. They then walked back toward the twirling lights of the police cars, knowing the demonic soul had finally vanished from their midst.

17

AFTERMATH

"How you feeling, Dempster?"

"Never better," he replied, tugging on his tie. "Thought I was a goner."

"We all did," said Coggs, placing his hand on his shoulder. "But I guess we got you to the hospital in time."

"Yep, I guess so."

"You did heal remarkably fast."

"Lucky she didn't sever anything," he said, running a hand through his graying hair.

Coggs looked at him for a moment. "Can't even see the scar," he said. "Your neck's completely healed as if it never happened."

"Just lucky, I guess."

Coggs nodded his head, and then began walking toward the black sedan. Dempster followed close behind.

"What've we got, John?" asked Dempster.

"Drug bust," he replied.

The two detectives slid inside the black car, and were soon screeching their way down the wide avenue.

"Any complications?" Dempster asked.

"Nah, just a normal bust," Coggs replied.

They could soon see the flashing police lights, and the cars blocking the street. Coggs pulled the car up to the curb, and turned off the engine. As they got out of the car, a police officer approached.

"Better stay alert," he told them. "They don't want to come out. We have a gun battle in progress."

Dempster looked at Coggs. "I'll go around the back," he said. "You take care of everything in front."

"You sure?"

"I'll be fine," Dempster answered.

Coggs watched as Dempster cut across the neighboring lawn, and vanished in the darkness.

"We've got to create a diversion for Dempster," Coggs said when he reached the other officers. They were kneeling behind the police cars, their guns out, ready to fire.

"He's going in there alone?" asked one of the officers.

"That's the way he wanted it," said Coggs. "Now get ready to start firing."

Coggs grabbed his gun, and then gave the word. The officers began firing shots at the house. In a matter of moments, shots were being fired back in their direction.

The firing continued, until suddenly there were screams coming from the house. The men inside the house stopped shooting, and then one of them suddenly leaped through the window to the grass below.

"What the hell is going on?" asked one of the officers.

"Don't know," Coggs replied. He stood there looking at the house, and then remembered something. "Dempster," he finally muttered.

As the police officers stopped shooting, another suspect came bounding through the window.

"Holy shit!" he screamed. "Don't let it get me!"

The officers rushed the house, and as they opened the door, they could see the dead bodies and the spreading puddles of blood. Coggs ran to the back of the house, attempting to find out what had happened to Dempster.

As he neared the opened back door, he could see a huge creature that looked something like a gigantic hyena slip into the darkness. He stood there, with wide eyes and open mouth, deciding not to follow.

Several minutes later, as Coggs and the police officers surveyed the slashed and mangled bodies, Dempster suddenly opened the front door and stepped inside the house.

"You all right, Dempster?" asked Coggs.

"Never felt better," the detective replied.

Coggs could see a blood spot on his white shirt.

"Were you hit?" he asked.

Dempster smiled. "Nah, they never touched me," he said, wiping his hand across the blood spot.

Coggs gazed at Dempster's hand. It was covered with what looked like animal hair.

"Did that creature do anything to you, Dempster?"

"What do you mean?"

"I mean, something attacked those perps inside that house."

Dempster grinned. "Yeah, but I'm on our side," he said.

Coggs looked at him. "I don't understand," he said. "How?"

"That female creature bit me," Dempster explained. "Well, now I'm one of them. But, this time, it'll be used for a good purpose."

"And you're okay with that?" Coggs asked.

"Never felt better," Dempster said with a smile.

Gail sat in her apartment thinking about Roger Kolak and all that had happened.

She looked down at her hand, and noticed that it was still bruised. It was a painful reminder of her struggle with Roger. She still couldn't believe he had become so evil before his death. She thought that he had even bitten her during one scuffle.

She sighed, and then heard the teakettle begin to whistle. Pouring herself a cup of hot tea, she walked back to the living room chair and sat down. For some reason, she felt rather nervous and began sipping her tea in an attempt to calm down. She glanced at the bite on her hand again, and frowned. Putting down her tea, she walked over to the window, and noticed that a gleaming full moon sat amid the gloomy darkness of the sky. She stared at it for a few moments, grimaced, and then walked back to the chair. Sitting down, she tried to relax.

She was about to take another sip of tea, when her hand began to shake. The tea began sliding from one end of the cup to the other, and then after a few more violent shakes, began spilling to the floor below. Gail felt as if she was losing control of herself, and then suddenly, she dropped the cup of tea. She heard it explode as it hit the floor, and then put a hand to her head, wondering what was wrong with her.

"My God," she muttered to herself. "I feel so weird."

She caught sight of her other hand, and noticed that it was covered with long, reddish hairs.

"What's wrong with me?" she asked herself, sitting up straight and trying not to panic.

She was about to stand up, and head to the bathroom, when her skin began to vibrate. She felt it bubbling up on her hands and shoulders, and then noticed the fine fur appearing on her arms and face. Her arms then began stretching, her shoulders began to bulge, and then she felt her neck begin to grow. Her breasts felt strange, and then began flattening against her chest.

"Oh, my God!" she screamed. "What's happening to me?"

The words came out in a rough, gravelly voice. She instinctively put her hands to her throat, and noticed they were now covered with thick, reddish tan hair. Before she could let out a scream, her head began distorting and hair began sprouting across her forehead. Fangs began to grow at the corners of her mouth, and her clothes began shredding as her muscles thickened.

Gail grunted and snarled, realizing she had become the tiger, the beast. Roger had infected her, and now she could do nothing about it. The desire for human flesh flashed through her brain, and she walked to the window and opened it.

A warm breeze rushed through the room. Gail sniffed at the air, and could smell human blood nearby. She then stepped outside onto the fire escape, and disappeared into the shadows of the night.